W9-CPB-553

Desire flashed through Nikos. Instant and insistent.

For a moment he felt consumed by it, overwhelmed. Then, with deliberate control, he subdued his reaction.

It was good that he desired her, it would make his task so much easier, but that was the only reason he should feel desire for her.

It was a means to an end, that was all—he had to remind himself of that, no matter how vulnerable she looked.

Harlequin Presents®

GREEK TYCOONS

They're the men who have everything—
except brides...

Wealth, power, charm—
what else could a handsome tycoon need?
In the GREEK TYCOONS miniseries you
have already met some gorgeous Greek
multimillionaires who are in need of wives.

Now meet the prosperous, striking and very
determined Nikos Kyriades in Julia James's
The Greek's Ultimate Revenge

This tycoon thought he could extract his revenge
without any feelings—only to learn how the
power of love can ignite a cold heart!

Don't miss the next book in this miniseries,

Bought by the Greek Tycoon
by Jacqueline Baird
#2512
January 2006

Julia James

THE GREEK'S ULTIMATE REVENGE

GREEK
TYCOONS

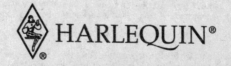

HARLEQUIN®

TORONTO • NEW YORK • LONDON
AMSTERDAM • PARIS • SYDNEY • HAMBURG
STOCKHOLM • ATHENS • TOKYO • MILAN • MADRID
PRAGUE • WARSAW • BUDAPEST • AUCKLAND

If you purchased this book without a cover you should be aware
that this book is stolen property. It was reported as "unsold and
destroyed" to the publisher, and neither the author nor the
publisher has received any payment for this "stripped book."

To my editor, Kim—
many, many thanks.

ISBN 0-373-12497-X

THE GREEK'S ULTIMATE REVENGE

First North American Publication 2005.

Copyright © 2004 by Julia James.

All rights reserved. Except for use in any review, the reproduction or
utilization of this work in whole or in part in any form by any electronic,
mechanical or other means, now known or hereafter invented, including
xerography, photocopying and recording, or in any information storage
or retrieval system, is forbidden without the written permission of the
publisher, Harlequin Enterprises Limited, 225 Duncan Mill Road,
Don Mills, Ontario, Canada M3B 3K9.

All characters in this book have no existence outside the imagination of
the author and have no relation whatsoever to anyone bearing the same
name or names. They are not even distantly inspired by any individual
known or unknown to the author, and all incidents are pure invention.

This edition published by arrangement with Harlequin Books S.A.

® and TM are trademarks of the publisher. Trademarks indicated with
® are registered in the United States Patent and Trademark Office, the
Canadian Trade Marks Office and in other countries.

www.eHarlequin.com

Printed in U.S.A.

PROLOGUE

'NIKOS! You've got to do something! You've got to! The little trollop has got her claws into Stephanos so deep he can't see straight!'

Nikos Kiriakis looked down at the woman lying in the hospital bed. She looked dreadful, and it stabbed at him painfully. Her face was pale and drawn, and she looked ten years older than her thirty-nine years. Though it had been only a minor operation medically, psychologically it had taken a much greater toll.

And, as if that wasn't enough, now it seemed her husband had chosen this moment of all times to be unfaithful.

Nikos's dark gold-flecked eyes hardened. His older sister had been a devoted wife to Stephanos Ephandrou—she didn't deserve this. Not now.

Not when a doctor had just told her that the results of a ~~py~~ were showing that both her Fall~~~~ ~~~~ly damaged. That her d~~~~

Stunned, Nikos had heard her out. Of all the men he knew, Stephanos Ephandrou had seemed to be the last husband to run a mistress. He had always been devoted to Demetria, had even said when he married her that he was glad her first marriage had borne no children rather than view it as what it was—a warning that perhaps all was not well with his twenty-nine-year-old bride's reproductive system.

Stephanos had married her after he'd finally persuaded her to divorce her chronically philandering first husband—her late father's choice for her, a socially suitable match for a Kiriakis, who had seen no reason to stifle his sexual proclivities on that account. And now it looked as if Stephanos was cut from the same cloth as Demetria's first husband—or worse. For what could be said about a man who was prepared to chase after another woman when his own wife was battling with infertility?

He lowered his tall frame, clad in an impeccably cut business suit, carefully onto the side of Demetria's bed. His handmade jacket eased across his broad shoulders as he took her hands, rubbing them gently.

are you sure you're not imagining

be so cruel, so dish

rible hope in her voice now. 'Women always fall at your feet. Always! Make this one do the same. Make her besotted with *you* so she leaves my Stephanos alone. Please, Nik, *please*!'

'I could speak to Stephanos,' he said slowly.

His answer was a violent shake of her head, panic in her eyes.

'No! No! I can't bear him knowing that I know. I can't. If you could only just get rid of her, get her claws out of him, he'd come back to me. I know he would. Oh, Nik, please. *Please!* If I could get pregnant—oh, dear heaven, if I could just get pregnant—then he'd be happy with me again! But if that harpy hangs on to him he'll never come back to me. Never!'

This was bad, thought Nikos. Demetria should not be upsetting herself like this, not at such a time. She'd been under such strain for so long, her desperation for a child eating into her.

But she was asking him to interfere in her marriage—come between a husband and his wife.

His expression tightened again suddenly. No, she was only asking him to come between a husband and his mistress...

A long, slow breath was exhaled from him as he soothed her hands.

His long lashes lowered over his eyes.

'What I can do, I will,' he promised her.

Her expression relaxed a fraction, the hectic look fading a little from her eyes.

'I knew I could count on you—I knew it!' There was relief in her voice now—relief and gratitude. 'You'll go right away, won't you, Nik? Won't you? You'll go and find her and get her claws out of Stephanos?'

'Very well.' His voice was sombre. Then he took another breath, quicker this time. 'But you, Demi, must promise me that you will start treatment immediately! No more prevaricating. The doctors have told you what can be done—there is considerable hope; you know there is. But these things take time—the doctors must have told you that—and you must delay no more.' His eyes narrowed suddenly. 'It might be a good idea,' he said slowly, 'to consult a fertility expert abroad—somewhere requiring quite a journey. Say, America. Get your doctor here to recommend someone in America. Tell Stephanos that he is the best and you insist on seeing him—and that he must come too. He will do that for you, I am sure. But I need time, Demi—you understand?'

Her eyes had lit up as she understood what he was suggesting. 'Sophia's daughter's wedding!' she added suddenly. 'I told her we couldn't come—but I think, oh, I really think that we might be able to make it after all. We could go on to Long Island after I've seen a consultant in New York.'

The hectic flush was fading now, and hope was filling her again—he could see it. She was speaking rationally—eagerly.

Her brother gave a tight smile.

'Two weeks. I need at least that long to do what you want,' he told her. 'Make sure Stephanos is away from Greece for two weeks. And Demi?' His eyes were hard. 'Keep him out of contact with the girl! I don't want her distracted.' His eyes hardened even more. 'Except,' he finished, his mouth twisting, 'by me.'

'Two weeks,' she promised him. Already her expression was less gaunt, her eyes less haunted. 'Oh, Nik,' she cried suddenly. 'You are the best, the very best of brothers! I knew you would help me. I knew it!'

As he handed Demetria over to the care of a nurse and left the private room, to stride on long legs down the lushly carpeted corridors of the exclusive clinic, his face grew grim. Stephanos was being a fool, all right. Even if he hadn't been married, and to a wife tormented by infertility, at fifty-two he had no business running after a girl of twenty-five. He was more than twice her age, for heaven's sake!

His expression darkened even more. But of course men in their fifties trying to recapture their youth were prime meat for girls like the one who had snared his brother-in-law. And if they were rich, as Stephanos Ephandrou undoubtedly was, they were even more attractive.

His eyes took on a cynical light. Well, if it was meat such girls wanted to feed on, then he was primest of the prime! On the Richter scale of desirable protectors he had to score even higher than Stephanos. His wealth was as great as Stephanos's, he had no inconvenient wife to circumvent, and, best of all, he was nearly twenty years younger than Stephanos.

He gave a cold, sardonic smile. Demetria had known exactly what she was doing when she'd turned to him for help—she knew very well what his reputation with her sex was. It was something she usually vigorously berated him over, as it came between her and her hopes for him finally marrying and settling down—as she longed, with sisterly affection, for him to do.

Well, he hadn't earned that reputation emptily—and now he could put it at his sister's service.

As he swung out of the clinic and climbed into his low-slung car, occupying one of the guest parking spaces, Nikos's face hardened.

Time to go and visit Miss Janine Fareham—a visit that he intended her to find quite, quite unforgettable. And one that would finish her affair with his brother-in-law once and for all.

CHAPTER ONE

JANINE eased herself over onto her stomach and sighed languorously, giving her body to the sun. In front of her the sunlight danced dazzlingly off the azure swimming pool. Beyond, slender cypresses pierced the cerulean sky.

The sound of children splashing and calling in the pool was the only noise. She felt the warmth of the sun like a blessing on her naked back.

The hotel was a haven of peace and luxury, brand-new, and Stephanos had shown it off to her with pride—the latest addition to his hotel empire.

A smile played around her lips.

Stephanos. It had been amazing, encountering him like that at Heathrow. He'd stopped dead, transfixed by her looks—and that had been it! He'd simply swept her off and taken her with him back to Greece. Her life would never be the same again.

A shadow flickered in her face. She just wished he could spend more time with her! Oh, he'd been completely honest with her, and she understood—of course she understood—that it was impossible for him to formally acknowledge her existence. All she could have of him would be snatched moments, all too brief. That was why he'd installed her here.

'Even if I cannot be with you, my darling girl, I want you to have the very best I can give you!' he had said to her.

She smiled fondly at the memory. Then the smile faded. His phone call last night, brief and hurried, as all his calls had to be, had not been good news. But she'd done her best to reassure him.

'I shall be fine,' she'd told him. 'You mustn't worry about me while you are in America.'

The trouble was, she thought ruefully, that Stephanos obviously *did* worry about her. His protectiveness was touching—he seemed so fearful that she would disappear from his life as unexpectedly as she had entered it. She smiled to herself again. He need have no fears. None at all. Nothing could part her from him now—she wanted to be part of his life for ever, however much of a secret it had to be.

She closed her eyes, letting the heat of the afternoon feed her drowsiness. For once she would enjoy this luxury beneath the golden sun.

So totally different from the life she usually led...

Nikos stood on the terrace, looking down over the pool. His eyes beneath the dark glasses were hard. So that was the girl, splayed out on a lounger. The girl who was wrecking his sister's marriage.

He paused a moment in the dappled shade, where the grapes were already ripening to a rich purple, and gazed down at her.

Emotions warred within him. The first was bitter anger—anger that the creature down there had the power to make Demetria weep in his arms, filled with despair.

The second was quite different.

She was, quite simply, delectable.

He had a vast experience of women, but this one was, he could see, in the very top rank. Her face was turned sideways, eyes closed, lashes lying long against her cheek as she lay relaxed on the lounger, but he could see that it was breath-catchingly lovely. A long, sun-bleached mane of pale hair swept across the pillow of the lounger, gently wisping across her smooth forehead. As for her body—

His eyes swept on, down the exposed length of her. She was naked apart from a tiny bikini bottom that barely covered her softly rounded cheeks. Her bikini top had been unfastened so that its ties would not mar the tanned perfection of her back. She did not look to be particularly tall, but she was very slender, with the kind of natural grace that girls of her age and type had in abundance.

She was sun-kissed, soft-limbed and sexy.

Oh, yes. Very, very sexy.

He could see immediately why Stephanos had not been able to resist her.

But Stephanos was married and should have *made* himself resist her. He, Nikos, was hampered no such impediment. Indeed, quite the opposite. He had given his betrayed sister his word on that.

His mission was very clear. He would quite deliberately, quite calculatingly, seduce Janine Fareham away from Demetria's husband.

Relief—no, more than relief eased through him. Satisfaction. Carrying out his mission would be no ordeal at all. In fact, he felt his body stir, and indulged it for a moment. It would be a positive pleasure.

For a brief while he let himself luxuriate in surveying her in all her enticing blonde beauty. Then, as he let his eyes feast on the nymph-like, softly rounded curves of her near naked body, as if a knife had come slicing down another image imposed itself, vivid and painful. His sister's gaunt, strained face as she begged him to help her sprang in front of his eyes.

His eyes hardened and he began to walk forward.

In her half-dozing state it took a moment for Janine to register that she could hear footsteps. A second later a shadow fell over her. Her eyes flew open and she looked up.

A man was standing there, looking down at her. He was very tall and dark. A generation younger than Stephanos. Was it one of the hotel staff? What did he want?

'*Kyria* Fareham?' The voice was deep and accented.

There was something about the tone that told her instinctively that this man was not a member of the hotel staff. This was a man who gave orders, not took them.

And he certainly didn't look like a guest either. Guests were all casually dressed—but this man was wearing an immaculately cut lightweight business suit and looked as if he had just walked out of a board meeting. Her eyes travelled on up to his face.

She felt her heartbeat lurch.

Eyes veiled by dark glasses bored down on her, surveying her as she lay there displayed for him. Suddenly she was acutely conscious that she was almost naked—and he was dressed in a formal suit. The disparity made her feel vulnerable, exposed.

Instinctively she pushed herself up to a sitting position, taking the sarong she'd been lying on with her, swinging her feet down to the warm paving. Even then she felt at a disadvantage. He still towered over her. For a Greek—and his looks and accent told her he had to be—he was very tall: easily six feet.

She stood up, knotting her sarong hurriedly around her in a fluid movement.

As her eyes focused on him properly she felt her breath catch. Her lips parted soundlessly, eyes widening.

She was looking at the most devastating male she had ever seen in her life.

What nature had bestowed on him his obvious wealth had accentuated. The superbly tailored suit fitted him like a glove, and she could see it had most definitely not been an off-the-peg purchase. But the man wearing it did not look off-the-peg either. He looked, she assessed instantly, *expensive*. His dark hair was expertly cut, feathering very slightly across his wide brow, and the dark glasses he wore did not need to have the discreet designer logo on them for her to know they had not been purchased from a market stall.

His nose was strong, and straight, with deep lines curving from it to the edges of his mouth.

His mouth—

Sculpted. That was the only word for it. With a sensuous lower lip she had to drag her eyes from, forcing herself to gaze into the blankness of his shaded regard.

There was something about this man that was making her heart race—and it was not just because he'd all but woken her out of a sun-beaten slumber. She felt the world shift around her and resettle.

As if something had changed for ever.

Then a different emotion surfaced. She'd been too busy gaping at this fantastic-looking man to take on board that he seemed to know who she was.

'Who wants to know?' She countered his enquiry warily. If he wasn't from the hotel who else knew she was here, except for Stephanos?

She pushed her hair back over her shoulders, feeling it tumbling warm and heavy down her back, and gazed at him, lips parted slightly.

Theos, thought Nikos, absorbing the sensuous gesture, she was perfect. Just perfect. The dream image of a sexy blonde.

But she wasn't cheap or tarty. Nothing so resistible! She was beautiful—head-turningly so. In an instant Nikos's expert eye took in the fact that she had one of those faces where every feature complemented every other, from her chestnut eyes, set in a heart-shaped face, to her generous mouth below a delicate nose. A golden tan gilded her flawless skin and her hair hung like pale spun gold down to her slender waist, faintly visible through the gauze of the turquoise sarong.

Desire flashed through him. Instant and insistent.

For a moment he felt consumed by it, overwhelmed. Then, with deliberate control, he subdued his reaction.

It was good that he desired her, it would make his task

so much easier, but that was the only reason he should feel desire for her. It was a means to an end, that was all, and the end was the removal—permanently—of this girl from his brother-in-law's marriage.

And to that end it was also necessary that this girl should be sexually vulnerable to him, Nikos. His eyes flickered over her again.

She was sexually aware of him all right. He knew the signs. Knew them well.

Beneath his regard Janine felt colour stealing out along her cheekbones. Heat flushing into her blood.

She could feel herself reacting to this man. She couldn't stop herself. There was something about him that was more than his devastating looks, more than that potent aura of wealth, or even the potent frisson of the power that a man like this must surely wield in the world he moved in. There was a raw sexuality beneath that tailored suit, hidden in those veiled eyes. She felt it licking at her.

Making her want him.

The realisation shocked her.

How could she be responding so strongly to a man she'd just set eyes on—whose eyes she couldn't even see yet? But she was, and she couldn't stop it. She felt her breasts tighten, her pupils flare, the colour flood to her cheeks.

Nikos watched her responding to him. That was good, very good. He wanted her responsive, wanted her physically aware of him—wanted her vulnerable to him.

There would be no problem seducing her, he knew.

Women came easily to him. They always had. Despite Demetria's bewailing, in his twenties he had indulged himself to the hilt. Now, in his thirties, he was more selective, preferring to choose women who could move in his world, who were sophisticated and discreet. Who understood what he wanted—and then moved on when he gave them the indication, as he always did.

Such women would neither know nor care that he was

about to make a temporary diversion, in a call of duty, to seduce away this female who threatened his sister's marriage, who was making a fool of a man who, up till now, he had always held in the greatest respect.

Now he let the female he was about to seduce, deliberately and calculatedly, respond to him, heighten her awareness of him, begin to make herself vulnerable to him.

He smiled.

Janine felt a kick go through her, powerful and shocking. The sculpted mouth parted, lines indenting around it, showing strong white teeth. It was an easy smile, yet it sent a frisson through her.

'We have a mutual—acquaintance,' he said, pausing minutely over the word. 'Stephanos Ephandrou.' He could see her stiffen fractionally as he dropped the name into the space between them.

'Oh?' responded Janine. Out of the blue he had mentioned Stephanos—what should she say? She knew Stephanos wanted her to be discreet about their relationship—yet here was a complete stranger who seemed to know there was a connection.

Her concern showed in her eyes. Nikos saw it and felt a stab of anger. Any lingering doubts he might have had that Demetria had somehow imagined her husband was having an affair vanished. The girl *was* carrying on with Stephanos. No doubt about it. His name had registered with her as loudly as if he'd rung a bell in her ear!

He forced his natural anger down. To display it now would ruin his strategy. Janine Fareham must have no idea of his hostility to her—indeed, she must think quite the opposite.

He bestowed another smile on her, and knew without vanity that it had distracted her attention from wondering why he seemed to know that she was connected to Stephanos Ephandrou.

He had been in two minds as to which approach to take

with her. He could, indeed, have simply engineered her acquaintance and set out to seduce her as a complete stranger. That approach had its advantages—it would have been simple and straightforward. But a female who made her living from the protection of rich, besotted older men might well be worldly enough to be wary of quick seductions that would jeopardise her lucrative relationship with her current protector. Instead, Nikos planned to use his acknowledged 'acquaintance' with Stephanos as a lever with which to gain the girl's confidence as swiftly as possible.

'Perhaps you will take a coffee with me and I can explain?' he went on, in that same smooth tone. He glanced towards the little poolside bar set back under the shade of some olive trees.

Still wary, but feeling she was being effortlessly manipulated by an expert, Janine let herself be ushered towards the seating area of the bar. It was a breath cooler under the trees, but she still felt her skin was flushed. The heat that was filling it, however, did not come from the sun.

She sat down on one of the canvas-backed chairs and the man did likewise, pausing only to beckon to the barman, who was already hurrying forward. Whatever it was that this man had, thought Janine, he had a lot of it! He wasn't the type to get ignored by a barman—or anyone else.

And certainly not women. Janine watched as a couple of female guests with small children in tow, seated at a table further off drinking fizzy drinks, immediately turned their heads in their direction. Their eyes were not for Janine. One of them said something to the other in Greek, and they laughed before turning their attention back to their children.

Janine didn't blame them for looking. The man sitting opposite her in his hand-tailored suit, would turn female heads wherever he went! Sexual magnetism radiated from him like a forcefield, pulling at everything in sight with a double X chromosome!

The barman was hovering, ready to take their orders.

'A frappe, please, no sugar,' requested Janine abstract-edly. She had already discovered that iced frappes were the ideal way to take coffee in the heat of the day, and were delicious and cooling. Her companion ordered coffee—Greek, she assumed.

The barman nodded acquiescently and hurried off.

Nikos turned his attention back to the girl. She was still wary, he could see—but still radiating sexual awareness. Not that she was flaunting her reaction to him. If anything, judging by the way she was sitting—pulled back in her chair, legs slanted neatly out of the way, her hand resting on the knot of her sarong, shielding her breasts—she was trying to conceal it.

Her lack of immediate sexual forwardness—despite his blatant appreciation of her charms—confirmed that he had been right to acknowledge Stephanos's presence in her life. The girl had landed herself a very soft number indeed—and she clearly realised it would be folly for her to risk her position as Stephanos's mistress, with all the guaranteed cashflow that it promised, for the sake of a brief interlude with a passing stranger. However much sexual pleasure she might gain from the encounter.

Hence her wariness.

Time to dispel it.

He slid his dark glasses off and slipped them into his jacket pocket. He relaxed back in his chair.

'Perhaps I should explain that I am here at Stephanos's suggestion,' he told her smilingly. 'Stephanos is a close friend and business associate, and when he heard I was coming to Skarios he suggested I stay at his hotel and asked me to seek you out,' he went on, the lie coming smoothly and fluently. He felt no guilt about lying to her. He only had to remember Demetria's tears and pleadings to absolve himself of all such guilt.

Janine made no answer. She was simply staring.

She felt her stomach clench. Dark, gold-flecked eyes

flickered over her, long lashes sweeping down over his cheeks. Her lips parted in a silent exhalation.

If she had thought his mouth hard to tear her gaze from, those eyes made such an act totally impossible. They were eyes she could drown in…making her feel weak…

For one long, endless moment she let herself gaze into those gold-flecked orbs, and felt her stomach churning like a cement mixer.

What was *happening* to her?

She'd *never* reacted this strongly to a man! Never! But this man—this complete stranger, whose name she didn't even know—was making the blood race in her veins, her face flush with heat…

Just by looking at her…

Their drinks arrived and she was grateful for the distraction. As the barman walked away she resisted the temptation to go back to gazing at the man opposite her, and instead forced herself to focus on what he had just said, not what he looked like.

'Stephanos asked you to seek me out?' she echoed dimly.

She sank back into gazing, riveted, into those magnetic, night-dark eyes.

They seemed to be looking into the heart of her. She felt herself go weak all over. All over again.

Nikos flashed another smile at her—and watched the girl's pupils flare.

'I hope you do not mind,' he said softly, 'that I have sought you out.'

His eyes rested on her and Janine felt her heart quicken. Oh, good grief, her bones were dissolving.… She just wanted to stare and stare.

Forcibly she dragged her mind back, fighting for composure. He seemed to be waiting for an answer.

'Oh—no. Of course not,' she managed to say. 'It's very good of you, Mr—er—?'

There was the slightest hesitation before Nikos spoke, but Janine did not notice it. Was quite incapable of noticing it.

'Kiriakis,' said Nikos smoothly. 'Nikos Kiriakis.'

Through veiled eyes he studied her for a reaction but saw none. The name meant nothing to her. He'd gambled that it wouldn't. Why should Stephanos talk about his brother-in-law to his mistress?

Nikos Kiriakis. Janine rolled the fluid syllables around in her head.

He was speaking again, and she brought her dazed attention back to what he was saying.

'Stephanos also had another suggestion,' Nikos went on, 'which for my part I would be very happy to comply with.' The lie rolled as smoothly as the first.

Janine stared. 'What suggestion?' Her voice still sounded totally abstracted.

Nikos was not offended. Usually he expected—and got— a hundred per cent attention from those he spoke to. But that Janine Fareham was incapable of bringing such focus to their conversation was only a good sign. A very good sign. He wanted her dazzled by him—lured by him.

'As you know, Stephanos is currently *en route* to the States,' began Nikos. He studied her reaction to this information—he calculated. Stephanos would have told her he was going to be abroad, although he doubted he would have told her that the reason for his sudden trip to New York was to take his wife to a fertility expert there.

'He is concerned that you may not have anything to do while he is away,' he continued. 'So he asked me if I would look after you while I am here—stop you getting bored.'

Janine's wandering thoughts snapped back. Suddenly the stomach-churning impact of Nikos Kiriakis's physical presence vanished. There was something far more important to focus on.

What had he just said to her? What was all that about Stephanos telling him she might be bored? Telling him to look after her? Surely, considering Stephanos's determination to keep her role in his life quiet, it was madness to send this Nikos Kiriakis to look her up?

Nikos saw the consternation in her face. It would not help his strategy.

'Perhaps I should tell you,' he said, his eyes resting on her, 'that, as a close friend of Stephanos Ephandrou, I am aware of the relationship between you, Ms Fareham—'

Her eyes widened, her consternation deepening.

'You *are*?'

CHAPTER TWO

OH, YES, thought Nikos savagely—that was good, Ms Fareham, that was very good! That little touch of surprise, and widening those big, beautiful eyes of yours. What the hell did you suppose everyone would think about your relationship with a fifty-two-year-old man? His mouth tightened.

She was sitting there, gazing at him, her eyes wide in her beautiful face. As if butter wouldn't melt in her mouth. As if neglected wives, heartbroken and despairing, had nothing to do with her. As if she were not responsible for his sister weeping in his arms.

The dark current of his anger surged dangerously near the surface. He forced it down. It had no part to play in his scheme now. The time for venting his anger on her would come later.

He made his mouth give a brief smile.

'Do not look so surprised. Such relationships are not unknown,' he remarked. For all his intentions, a sardonic tone was audible in his voice. He took a mouthful of coffee, then set back his cup with a click on the metal surface of the table.

Janine eyed him cautiously. Stephanos had urged such discretion that she was taken aback by this man calmly referring to it. But then, she reasoned, presumably such relationships were not unusual. Especially not with non-Greek women, with their more relaxed attitude to sexual behaviour. Clearly Nikos Kiriakis saw nothing exceptional about it.

Even so, it was disconcerting to hear this complete stranger refer to it. Although, of course, she realised belat-

edly, he wasn't a stranger to Stephanos. It was odd that
they were friends, though—Nikos Kiriakis was easily a generation younger than Stephanos. He didn't look much over
thirty, really. Thirty-five at the most. He was certainly in
incredible physical condition…

'Please don't look so alarmed,' he went on, the smooth
note back in his voice. 'I appreciate that Stephanos wishes
to be discreet about your relationship. It is very understand-
able. You may be assured of my discretion.' He smiled
again, a warm, reassuring smile, and she felt suddenly
breathless.

'So,' said Nikos, knowing he had overcome that barrier
successfully, 'would you care to undertake a little sightsee-
ing? It would be very useful to me as, amongst other business matters, I am here to see whether this island would be
suitable for a summer villa for myself.'

That was true enough, he thought. From what little he'd
seen of the island firsthand so far, and from what Stephanos
had already told him, it might well be suitable. The most
southerly of the Ionian islands, Skarios was dryer and hotter
than the others, and far less developed. The airport had
recently been extended to allow tourist planes to land, but
there was general agreement that any development should
be both upmarket and sympathetic to the landscape—like
his brother-in-law's luxury hotel, which had been designed
to be low-rise and traditionally styled.

'Well,' he went on, 'what do you think?'

About what? thought Janine, trying to drag her mind
back, because she had resumed gazing raptly at the incredible man sitting opposite her.

'Showing me the island?' he prompted, well aware of the
reason for her vagueness, and well pleased by it. Her reaction was exactly what he'd hoped it would be.

Janine felt her breath catch. Those gold-flecked eyes were
resting on her, making her feel…feel…

Breathless. Totally breathless.…

'What do you say?' pursued Nikos. He was in no doubt as to her answer. Not in the slightest.

'It sounds wonderful!' said Janine, unable to stop herself sounding enthusiastic.

Suddenly Nikos Kiriakis's arrival could not have seemed more timely.

Stephanos had extracted a reluctant promise from her not to hire a car and explore the island herself—'The roads are far too dangerous!' he'd said anxiously—which had left only the not very appealing prospect of taking taxis or restricting herself to the very limited tour buses.

She'd be an idiot to turn down the opportunity of keeping company with the most breathtaking man she'd ever set eyes on...

Careful, a voice inside her cautioned. This Nikos Kiriakis might be gorgeous, but, believe me, he has the same effect on every female he comes across. Just because he eyed you up it doesn't mean you should start getting ideas.

She sobered. Anyway, this isn't a good time for getting ideas like that. This time should be devoted to Stephanos.

But Stephanos isn't here...and he's sent Nikos Kiriakis to me...

To show you around, stop you getting bored, she reminded herself acidly. Nothing else...

He was talking again, and she brought her mind back with a snap.

'Good. Then we are agreed. We shall make our first excursion tomorrow!' There was satisfaction in his voice. He had made contact, and got her agreement—incredibly easily!—to spend time with him alone. Now it was time for the next step in his carefully planned campaign.

'For today—' he shot back his cuff and glanced at the gold watch circling his wrist '—it is too late to make any kind of expedition. Besides—' the smile quirked again '—I have only just flown in from Athens, and that pool looks far too inviting to resist.' He frowned, as his gaze took in just how thronged with children it was. 'Perhaps it will get quieter later.'

'Yes, it empties out around six-ish,' confirmed Janine. Her spirits were zipping around in her, whooshing like crazy. 'The sea is a better bet right now. A path goes down to the beach just beyond the pool.' She indicated with her hand.

He nodded. 'The sea it shall be, then,' he said. His eyes swept over her once more. 'Perhaps you would care to join me there later when you have finished your sunbathing?'

Janine's eyes flickered. 'Thank you—yes.'

Her voice was still breathless, and she felt light-headed.

Nikos got to his feet. 'I'll see you down there,' he told her, and bestowed one last smile on her for good measure before he walked away towards the hotel.

Janine gazed after him until he disappeared from view.

Slowly, she bent her head to drink her frappe through the twin straws in the glass.

Her pulse was racing.

Nikos plugged his laptop cable into the wall-jack in his room and dialled into his e-mail. As he waited for his latest messages to download, the image of Janine Fareham floated enticingly in his mind. He let himself indulge in recollecting her charms, plentiful as they were, and replayed the exchange he had had with her.

Satisfaction filled him. Things were going exactly to plan. She was responding to him very satisfactorily.

And you are responding to her—definitely responding…

But that was good, he reasoned immediately. It was good that he should feel such desire for a woman he needed to seduce. It would lend great verisimilitude to the undertaking.

And danger?

He rebuffed the notion immediately. What danger was there for him in this enterprise? None. He would seduce

Janine Fareham, enjoy her—because she looked as if she were going to be very enjoyable indeed—and that would be that. She would not be returning to Stephanos.

Without conceit he knew that he had a lot more to offer than a man of Stephanos's age! And even if she thought she could go back she would discover otherwise. Once Stephanos knew of her defection there would be no way that he would take her back after she had fallen into his, Nikos's, bed!

No, his plan was entirely without danger—least of all to himself. Janine Fareham was a stunningly attractive female, and he would certainly enjoy taking her to bed—but then he always enjoyed taking beautiful women to bed.

And so many were so willing…

A caustic smile parted his lips. Demetria might volubly yearn for the day she saw him finally married, and berate him for his sexual lifestyle, but it was hardly a problem for him. The stream of women wanting him to desire them was endless, so even if he did tire of them—as he always did— it caused him no difficulty. He simply moved on to the next one.

There was always a next one.

And there would certainly be another one once he had finished with his brother-in-law's mistress.

Irritated with himself for giving form to such pointless musing, he stabbed at the mouse button to open the first e-mail his PA had forwarded as worthy of his attention. In an instant his mind was preoccupied, diverted totally on to business matters.

By the time he had surfaced from his business affairs, the sun was setting. The room temperature was pleasantly cool, thanks to the background air-conditioning, but when he stepped out onto the wide balcony of his room the afternoon warmth enveloped him. Even without his jacket he was far too hot.

Returning indoors, he stripped off and donned a pair of

swimming trunks, before reaching for a pair of crisply cut cotton shorts and a casual shirt. As he reached for a beach towel the image of Janine Fareham in her skimpy bikini wafted once more through his mind. She would be waiting for him by now, no doubt.

Time to go to work.

At the bottom of the flight of steps that cut into the rock between the gardens and the sea he paused, looking around him. To one side of the hotel beach and further out to sea the windsurfers were clearly in action, skimming and twisting over the surface of the water. Immediately in front of him were two rows of loungers and parasols, and a bar café was set back from the beach, to save guests having to go back up to the pool level.

Out to sea, the westering sun was turning the water to turquoise.

He could see no sign of the girl.

And then he spotted her.

She was out to sea, swimming offshore in a leisurely breast-stroke. Her hair, he could just tell at this distance, seemed to be knotted on her head, out of the water.

Casting around to see which lounger she had taken, he saw the beach bag she'd had up by the pool and walked across to toss his towel down on it. Then he undressed down to his trunks to wade into the water. It caressed him like silk, and, with a lithe movement, he dived forward, striking out to sea in a powerful, fast stroke.

He closed the distance between the shore and the girl in a few moments, and then went right on past her. He needed exercise after the inactivity of the day. Besides, the vigorous exercise would help to drain off that layer of submerged, persistent anger he had felt ever since Demetria had dropped her bombshell. It wouldn't drain out completely, of course. Nothing could make it do that until the cause of his anger was removed. But he knew he had to keep his feelings under tight control—he must not, *must not*, let it show. Janine Fareham must get no inkling of it—not until it was far, far too late for her.

Just thinking of her, of the pain she was causing Demetria, the damage she was doing to Stephanos's marriage, made the anger surge through him again. It flared through him, urging his muscles forward, pushing him past the pain barrier as he churned through the water at a punishing speed.

Only when he was several hundred metres out to sea did he finally slow, his burst of energy and aggression spent. He turned over onto his back, temporarily exhausted, floating on the swell of the sea for a while, letting his heart-rate slow and his muscles recover.

His anger seemed abstract now, far away. Demetria and her suffering seemed far away too. Another image formed in his mind. The image of a beautiful blonde with a sun-kissed body and softly rounded limbs.

The woman he was going to calculatedly and deliberately seduce—because she was his sister's husband's mistress.

For a few brief seconds another emotion surfaced. An alien one. Unwelcome.

Reluctance.

Reluctance at the task ahead of him.

And reluctance to question why he felt that way. What was wrong with what he was planning to do? The girl was threatening to destroy his sister's marriage—he was simply trying to help Demetria, who had quite enough torment in her life coping with her infertility. She did not need her husband cheating on her with a younger woman!

And just because, he reminded himself tightly, the younger woman in question had turned out to be so incredibly desirable, that was no reason to flinch from what he had promised Demetria he would do. No reason to feel reluctant to pursue his carefully planned strategy of calculated seduction.

He put his reluctance aside. There was no reason why he

should not do what he was setting out to do. The girl had got her claws into his brother-in-law—he was going to remove them. End of story. He had set out on this course and he would pursue it to the end. He would accomplish what he had set out to do—what he knew he had to do.

And use whatever it took to achieve that goal.

There was nothing else to be done.

He flipped over and headed back to shore with a steady, unhurried stroke, making for the girl who was his target and his mission. She too had circled round to head back towards the beach, still kicking with her leisurely breast-stroke, head held high out of the water. As he neared her he dived and swam underwater for some metres, emerging just in front of her in a shower of spray.

Janine's breast-stroke stalled abruptly. She'd been miles away mentally, using the smooth, rhythmic movement of her body in the sea to let her mind drift miles away.

But not too many miles. Just as far as the memory of the man whose face had been burning into her retinas since she had laid eyes on him. Once he'd disappeared from view, heading back up to the hotel, she'd gone back to her pool lounger and scooped up her things, heading down to the beach.

She'd tried to sunbathe again, but it had been impossible. Impossible to relax. She'd been fizzing with electricity—electricity generated by Nikos Kiriakis.

She'd given up trying to relax and instead had knotted up her hair, retied her bikini straps firmly, and gone into the water. Here, cool blue satin slipping past her heated body, she had given herself to the indulgence of recalling every last detail of the most breathtaking man she'd ever laid eyes on.

And suddenly now here he was, in the flesh, beside her.

And such flesh…

They were both out of their depths, still treading water, but the translucent liquid did little to hide from her the power and perfection of his body. Broad, bare shoulders topped a muscled chest, fuzzed with hair, every ab and pec lovingly outlined. No wonder he'd been able to swim at speed! His body was in superb condition.

Just like the rest of him…

His dark, wet hair was slicked back from his face. Diamonds glittered on those lush, long lashes of his.

White teeth flashed in a grin.

'If you swam any slower you'd go backwards!' said Nikos Kiriakis to her teasingly.

Janine trod water, trying to regain her composure and trying not to stare open-mouthed at Nikos Kiriakis with hardly a stitch on him.

'You go ahead,' she managed. 'I'll catch you up.'

He gave a laugh and swam away. Janine watched him carve through the water.

Like a shark, she thought…

Lean, dark and dangerous…

Now, why should she think that? What was dangerous about Nikos Kiriakis? He was a fantastic-looking male, but that was the only dangerous thing about him—and it was a danger every female who set eyes on him would experience.

A danger that she would end up doing something totally stupid over him.

Her lips pressed together. Well, *she* was not stupid. She'd got this far in life by not being stupid—not in the way that the likes of Nikos Kiriakis made women stupid. Women like her mother. Always falling for a handsome face. Oh, her mother had thought it 'romantic' to have one fervid affair after another, but Janine had never seen it like that. And where had it got her mother? Louise's flitting butterfly existence, lover after lover, had been a gilded existence, filled with nothing but parties and self-indulgence. Filled with men like Nikos Kiriakis.

She knew what men like Nikos Kiriakis were like. They were too rich, too handsome, too damn sexy to be anything but bad. And Nikos Kiriakis was definitely bad. He would be used to women swooning at his feet in droves!

Well, she mustn't be one of them.

She made a face.

She didn't need to tell herself that! Didn't need to warn herself. Nikos Kiriakis had the seal of approval from Stephanos—he wasn't going to be any kind of danger. OK, so he'd eyed her up, but that didn't mean anything. And she'd eyed *him* up—it had been impossible not to. But that didn't mean anything either. She wouldn't let it.

Her impeccable logic as to her own state of safety from Nikos Kiriakis lasted as long as it took to follow him to shore. By the time she was wading out of the water he had already towelled himself dry and had calmly appropriated her lounger. Nikos lay back and let her look, hands behind his head, shoulders slightly raised by the adjustable head-rest, and he was subjecting her to a long and thorough examination.

In the space of less than a second Janine felt more aware of her body than she had ever felt in her life. And of just how close to being totally naked she was.

Suddenly, from being a quite unexceptional item of swimwear, her bikini seemed to shrink on her body, clinging damply to her tautened breasts and barely concealing her pubis.

As for the rest of her, every inch of flesh was totally exposed to him.

And every inch of it tingled as if an electric current were passing through it.

Every step she made to her lounger, she felt that dark, gold-flecked gaze resting on her appraisingly.

Being able to seize her towel and wrap it around her like a cocoon was a moment of exquisite relief. And then, just like a switch being thrown, she realised that she had become the one doing the appraising.

He lay back and let her look.

Oh, she didn't do it as blatantly as he had her, he acknowledged. She made some pretence of unknotting her hair and shaking it loose. But he could see perfectly well that her eyes were fixed on him, covertly working over him through those long lashes of hers. Working over his body.

Well, that was good. That was very good. He wanted her to like what she saw. Wanted her to want him.

It made him want her too…

With a sudden movement he jack-knifed to his feet. It took a lot of control to make it look like an intentional movement.

Where the hell had that come from? The strength and immediacy of his reaction to her perusal shocked him.

With iron discipline he crushed his response. A public beach was not the place for it!

Immediately his imagination leapt to provide another venue—one where his reaction would be exactly what he wanted. A private beach—just the two of them—and Janine Fareham raising her arms to let the golden fall of her hair cascade over her bared breasts…

Again he crushed his response, forcing himself to regain control.

'Here,' he said, gesturing at the lounger he'd just vacated. 'This was yours. I'll use this one.'

He turned to the adjacent lounger, flicking his towel over it. But his gesture went unappreciated.

'I think I'll head back,' replied Janine. Her voice was not quite steady, she noticed, and it dismayed her. She mustn't react like this to this man. She just mustn't! 'I'll take a shower and wash off the salt.'

She flickered a smile at him, not meeting his eye, and grabbed her bag, stuffing her feet into her beach sandals haphazardly. She had to get out of here—fast.

Behind her, Nikos watched her hurry off, his eyes narrowing. Then, slowly, he lowered himself back down on the lounger, gazing blindly out to sea. OK, so she could turn him on. Fast.

Quite something for a man of his experience.

And very enjoyable…

And dangerous?

He frowned.

But it was good. That he was responding to her sexually like this. After all, he reasoned, he had to make this deliberate seduction of his look real. Convincing.

Convincing? He'd damn near convinced everyone on the entire beach!

With a rasp of irritation he pushed the mocking comment aside. It wasn't helpful. Instead he made a lightning review of the situation—the same as he would if this were a business deal he was pushing through. OK, so where was he on this?

Fact: he needed to get Janine Fareham into bed with him ASAP. The sooner she was in, the sooner she'd be out. And out of Stephanos's bed as well.

Fact: Janine Fareham turned him on.

Fact: that was good. Very good. Just as he could leverage *her* desire for *him*, so he could leverage *his* desire for *her*. The more leverage, the sooner he'd achieve his goal.

Saving Demetria's marriage.

Because that, and only that, was the object of this exercise. Enjoying Janine Fareham in bed was nothing more than incidental to that objective.

He'd better not forget it.

He closed his eyes. The westering sun was warm on his bare, damp skin.

Might as well catch some rays and chill out. Take a break before Act II of his fast-track seduction of Janine Fareham got underway.

He let his muscles relax.

It had been a long day. A long week. A long month. In fact it was a long time since he'd simply relaxed in the sun like this. Doing nothing. Letting the light breeze play over his body, the sun bathe his skin.

No one could contact him, no one could make demands on him. He didn't need to check e-mails, or stock prices, or take conference calls.

He could just stay totally out of touch and let the world outside take care of itself.

Time enough to pursue and put paid to Janine Fareham.

Right now he felt like relaxing.

Halfway up, the stone steps widened into a little parapet, affording a view down to the beach through the vegetation. Janine paused. She couldn't resist looking back.

Immediately she saw him. He'd occupied the other lounger and was lying there, hands behind his head, face tilted into the sun. She let her eyes move over his body. From here, at this safe distance, she could let herself do that. Let her eyes run over the smooth, bronzed, muscled torso, down over the taut, tight abs, and pick out the darker arrow that disappeared under the drawstring of his trunks. For a second her gaze lingered, then hastily moved on, down over the powerful hair-fuzzed thighs and down the long length of his legs.

He did not move—lay there completely motionless.

He looked, she thought, like a leopard drowsing in the sun.

The little shiver came again, that disturbing eddy that set her nerves tingling.

She wanted to go on gazing at him.

No! With an effort she pulled away, pushing back from the wooden railing that edged the pathway. Resolutely she twisted around and went on up the steps, not looking back.

The pool area was emptying now, much quieter. She did not linger but made her way indoors, her sandals flapping on the stone tiles, under the arching honeysuckle whose fragrance caught at her. Inside the hotel it was cooler, but only just. Her room was much colder, chilly even, with its background air-conditioning.

For the next hour she occupied herself showering, washing her hair, giving herself a facial and manicure, washing out her underwear, and finally pulling a sundress over her head. She phoned Room Service for coffee and watched an international news channel on television until it arrived. Then, tray in hand, she went out onto her balcony.

The sun was nearly setting now, licking the sea with gold. Janine sat herself down at the little table, stretching out her legs as she poured her coffee. Her still damp hair curled around her shoulders and she idly fingered it as she sipped her coffee, gazing out over the view.

It certainly was a fantastic setting for a hotel. From here the sea spread out before her as far as the eastern coast of Sicily. She sat and watched the sun slipping over the horizon, silhouetting the tall cypress trees, sure that she could see Pheobus's fiery chariot pulling the sun to its watery bed.

A strange, powerful feeling went through her. My first visit to Greece, she thought. All these years and I've never been here. Never known why it's so emotional a place for me.

Her thoughts slipped to Stephanos. If he wasn't in New York yet he must be very shortly, surely. He seemed very far away. Very distant from her.

Something—she did not know what—made her glance down, over the hotel gardens. Someone was strolling around the edge of the pool, shirt pulled on but unbuttoned, towel casually slung over his shoulder.

Nikos Kiriakis.

Hastily, lest he suddenly glance up and see her looking down at him, she dipped her head, pouring out more coffee. By the time she had lifted the cup to drink from it he had reached the hotel and she could see him no more.

The phone rang in her room some twenty minutes later. She was reading her book still out on the warm balcony, though she could hardly see to read any more. Already the lights in the gardens had been illuminated, including those in the pool, which glowed brilliantly. People had started to stroll out for the evening, making their way to the pool bar for a drink before dinner. Children's voices piped.

She would have an early dinner in the buffet dining room, where all the families ate with their children. Nikos Kiriakis would doubtless eat much later, and in the à la carte dining room reserved for adults.

The soft beeping of the phone interrupted her. Assuming it was Reception, she was completely unprepared for the dark, liquid tones of Nikos Kiriakis in her ear.

'I've reserved a table for nine. I'll meet you on the terrace at half past eight. Does that give you enough time to be ready?'

There was a note of humour in the voice, as though its owner were acknowledging that a woman needed a large amount of time to be ready to dine.

It took Janine a good few seconds to gather her wits. Even then she sounded no better than half-witted.

'Um—you don't have to reserve tables. You just wander in whenever you want. The buffet runs till ten.'

'We are not dining in the buffet restaurant.' The smile in his voice was even more pronounced now. 'Fond as I am of children, I prefer something a little more peaceful for dinner.'

'Please—you don't have to ask me to dinner.' The words blurted from her.

'But I would like very much to dine with you, Janine,' replied Nikos. 'So I look forward to seeing you at half past eight, *ne*?'

He rang off, giving her no chance to argue the point any more. For a moment she stood there, receiver in hand. Feeling dazed.

She bit her lip. The way he had looked at her as she

came out of the water sprang vivid in her mind. The way he had looked at her when she'd been lying by the pool. The way he had looked at her at the pool bar.

It doesn't mean squat! He's the kind of male who does that to every female. And every female does it back to him. I bet you every single female head will turn when he walks into the dining room tonight—and so what? He's only having dinner with you because of Stephanos. Got it?

She drew in her breath and felt better.

Promptly, a different cause for anxiety assailed her. She hurried over to her wardrobe and flung it open, staring at the contents.

She didn't have a thing to wear! Not for dinner in the à la carte restaurant! When Stephanos had been here she hadn't really bothered much with anything other than the expensive beachwear he'd bought her from the hotel's boutique. It had been perfectly OK to wear a long hibiscus-print wrap-around skirt and matching bolero top when she'd spent time in his suite.

But the à la carte restaurant was sophisticated and glizty—and her wardrobe definitely wasn't!

For a moment it seemed like fate. No suitable clothes, therefore a sign that she should not dine with Nikos Kiriakis. She would dial Reception and get them to put her through to his room, and she would make her excuses.

Or, of course, she could simply go down to the hotel boutique and buy something that *would* pass muster...

The boutique certainly did stock evening wear. Very expensive evening wear too. But then those who could afford to stay here could afford those prices. Not that she would have to pay—Stephanos had made it clear she could get anything she wanted from the hotel's select collection of shops and simply charge it to her room.

With sudden decision, she fetched her room key and set off for the boutique.

*　　*　　*

Nikos glanced at his watch. She was late. Well, that was no surprise. Women usually were. He sipped his beer contemplatively, eyes scanning the gardens, artfully spotlit here and there, and splashed with light from the pool's underwater lighting.

There was a swish of skirts, and someone hurried up to the table.

'I'm sorry I'm late!' The voice sounded slightly breathless.

He turned his head.

Slowly, very slowly, he drank her in. He felt his gut kick as if in slow motion.

She looked—breathtaking!

And as he slowly, very slowly, exhaled he realised that that was exactly what she had done. Taken his breath away.

She was wearing saffron. It shouldn't have gone with her fair hair and golden looks. It was a colour meant for a Greek complexion, dark hair, dark eyes.

Yet on this particular blonde it looked, quite simply, ravishing.

It was chiffon, layers of it, and it seemed to float, skimming over that beautiful body of hers like a kiss. Her hair was caught up—not in a rough-and-ready knot, the way it had been when she was swimming—but in an elegant, flawless style that lent her height and grace. A few tendrils whispered at her face, the nape of her neck.

He felt himself relax back in his seat as he drank her in.

Tiny earrings glinted at her lobes. Gold, like the delicate chain that encircled her neck, and each wrist. Her waist was very slender—he could have spanned it with his hands. The bones of her shoulders were exquisitely sculpted. Her neck was graceful, holding her head poised, erect.

Her eyes were deepened by make-up, her mouth accentuated with lipstick, the colours toning with the saffron. Her cheekbones seemed higher than they had been—more artful make-up, he surmised. A scent came from her—a light, haunting fragrance.

It caught at him.

She caught at him.

Slowly, he got to his feet.

'Won't you sit down?'

Janine took her place. Her breathing was quick, and shallow. It was because she'd been rushing, she told herself. Rushing ever since she'd realised that she'd taken ages and ages in the boutique, trying on just about every evening dress they'd had in her size. The assistant had been very patient, assuring her that the shop would not close until late that night, and that she could take all the time she wanted.

Choosing had been impossible—she didn't know why, but it had. In the end she'd followed her instinct, not her reason, and gone for the saffron. Her reason had told her that it should be worn by someone with much darker, more dramatic colouring than she possessed, but there had been something about the way the dress felt on her, whispered over her flesh, that had made her know that this was the one she wanted. So eventually, having tried on everything else again, she'd gone back to the saffron.

And now she was getting proof that she'd made the right choice!

With that same quick breathing she settled into her chair. Her dining partner was not wearing a suit, but his open-necked shirt was clearly not off the peg. It clung with tailored perfection to his broad shoulders, smoothing down over his torso, exposing the strong column of his throat.

She dragged her eyes away and let herself meet his gaze. He was sitting looking at her, and appreciating everything he saw!

'Hi,' she said idiotically. She had to recover her composure. She had to appear normal. Right now she was having palpitations like some Victorian maiden!

'*Kalispera,*' replied Nikos, his voice soft with amusement.

He liked what he saw—he liked it a lot. Oh, not just the exquisite appearance of this extraordinarily beautiful girl, but the fact that she was so clearly responding to him, and the way he was looking at her.

A waiter was there, hovering discreetly, but attentively.

'What would you like to drink?' Nikos asked her.

For a moment she wanted to say *Something strong, to calm my nerves*, but then she realised that strong liquor was the last thing she should drink right now. So instead she murmured, 'Oh, orange juice, please.'

He raised a slight eyebrow at this, and she went on lightly, 'To go with my frock!'

A smile indented his mouth and he nodded, relaying the order to the waiter in Greek—unnecessary though it was, since the hotel staff all spoke English. The man disappeared.

'It's extremely beautiful.' Nikos indicated her dress with a slight inclination of his head.

'I got it from the boutique just now. That's why I'm running late!'

She could hear her own breathlessness in her voice. It annoyed her—alarmed her. She was sounding like some wet-behind-the-ears teenage girl on her first date! It was ridiculous.

But the thing was she *did* feel like a teenager again! Excitement was running through her, and it was because of the man sitting opposite her. She could tell herself all she liked that Stephanos had simply sent him to babysit her, but her body wasn't taking that on board. Her body was shimmering like a fairy light on a Christmas tree!

'It was worth the wait,' said Nikos. He let his eyes wash over her again, to confirm his words.

The waiter's arrival with her glass of freshly squeezed orange juice was a reprieve, and she sipped eagerly. Then the *maître d'* arrived with two large leatherbound menus, bowing copiously to Nikos and running through the specialities of the day in rapid Greek.

Janine gazed down virtually blindly at the menu, forcing herself to read the words. As the *maître d'* bowed one last time, and glided away, Nikos listed the day's catch.

'Oh, not calamari!' Janine exclaimed. 'It's the suckers on the tentacles. They're disgusting!'

Nikos laughed. 'It can be served without those appendages,' he assured her. 'Have you not eaten squid yet?'

Janine gave an exaggerated shudder.

'I'll stick to real fish, please.'

She settled on red mullet, with a seafood terrine to start, and closed the menu. She gazed out at the gardens.

'Isn't it the most beautiful place?' she sighed. A wonderful feeling of well-being was suffusing her. It was everything—the beautiful gardens, the soft Mediterranean night and, above all, the presence of Nikos Kiriakis sitting opposite her, drawing her eye inexorably to him.

'The view is certainly quite stunning,' her companion murmured.

She glanced back to smile at him—and saw that he was not looking out over the gardens at all. Instead, his dark eyes were fixed on her face, and there was an expression in them she'd have had to be blind not to recognise...

She felt the colour run again, and hastily took a drink.

Nikos watched her reach for her glass. For a woman who made her living out of the touch of wealthy men, she really was remarkably unflirtatious. Perhaps, he found himself thinking, that was her allure. That she did not come on to her targets—she let them come on to her.

After all, she was so very much worth coming on to...

Emotions twisted inside him.

She might be sitting there, with a beauty as breathtaking as it was alluring, but it did not—could not—take away what she did, what she used that beauty for. That was what he had to remember. And her looks were of interest to him for one reason only—they would make his seduction of her palatable to him. He would get his revenge for the pain she was causing his sister.

He let his gaze rest on her, with the eyes of a connoisseur. She really was extraordiny. Some women couldn't make the transition from bikini to evening gown—but she could. By the pool and on the beach, she had looked sexy and sun-kissed. Now she looked graceful and soft, like a gazelle—her slender neck, her parted lips, the soft swell of her breasts beneath the chiffon of her dress.

As he watched he could see her nipples just graze against the filmy material, each one outlined for him.

All he had to do was reach out his hand, and touch with the tips of his fingers. Close his palm over their sweet ripeness…

Like a sheet of flame, desire sucked at him. Wanting to be sated. Now. Right now.

With visible effort he slammed down on his reaction.

He felt shaken.

Just as on the beach, his reaction had come out of nowhere, like a flashflood, thundering suddenly through his veins. Desire—hot, tearing, urgent. And out of control.

With gritted teeth he dragged back control over his body, his reaction. What the hell was he doing?

He was acting like a man besotted, and with some foxy little piece like Janine Fareham.

Yes, that was what he had to remember! That Janine Fareham used men's desires for her own ends—to buy gowns like the one she was displaying her body in tonight! He let his anger at her, deep and unrelenting and unforgiving, seep back, filling him like a dark tide. That was the only response he should be having to her. Oh, sexual desire, yes—but at *his* bidding, not hers. Under *his* control, not hers.

He relaxed again, back in control of his reaction to her.

He would take Janine Fareham, possess her and enjoy her.

And then get rid of her from his life—and Stephanos's life.

A line from Shakespeare snaked into his mind—'I'll have her, but I'll not keep her long.'

It would do very well for Janine Fareham.

Janine carefully removed some bones from her fish and took a forkful of the delicious dish. It was weird. She seemed hyper-aware of every movement she made. Aware of everything.

Especially Nikos Kiriakis. In its own disturbing way, dining with him was nerve-racking. She wanted to do nothing more than just sit there and stare at him open-mouthed. But she knew she could not. Must not. Instead she had to make conversation, or rather let him make conversation, and she had to respond as if she had her brain in place, instead of just wanting to gaze and gaze at him. She had to chat away—talking about innocuous subjects, like what there was to see on Skarios, and what kind of villa he was interested in buying, and things like snorkelling and windsurfing.

Not that she wasn't grateful for the ordinariness of the conversation. She didn't think she could deal with anything more.

Windsurfing was nice and safe, and since it was something she knew nothing about it meant she didn't really have to do anything other than prompt with a question and Nikos Kiriakis would do all the talking. So she could sit there, chin on her hand, and indulge herself wondering just what it was about his eyes that were so compelling, watching how his mouth moved when he talked, and how his dark, silky hair shaped his beautiful face...

Anyway, windsurfing wasn't something she'd ever had a go at. It seemed very strenuous, and everyone she saw doing it seemed to be very good—which was pretty off-putting, considering how useless she knew she would be. She was bound to spend most of her time falling off the board in a very undignified way. Nikos Kiriakis, it seemed, judging by his enthusiasm and knowledge, was a keen exponent. She was not surprised. He hadn't got that muscle tone from sitting behind an executive desk all his life!

Thinking about Nikos Kiriakis's body was not a good idea—it brought too many images vividly to mind. Instead, she watched his lean, strong hands move salt cellars and cutlery into position on the white damask tablecloth as he explained the mysteries of tacks and gybes, wind speed and board directions.

He paused and looked at her expectantly. She sighed and shook her head.

'It's no good. I'm totally lost. I think I'd rather just waft along on a boat, really.'

He gave a laugh. 'You don't do much wafting when you're crewing on a yacht!'

'I was thinking of something that had an engine and didn't require any work on my part,' she responded lightly.

'You enjoy not working?' There was nothing in his voice, his expression, to indicate anything more than a light-hearted riposte, yet there was something…perhaps in his eyes…

'Who doesn't?' she answered, just as lightly. 'And right now,' she went on, 'I definitely don't feel like working. I'm on holiday!'

For a second that fleeting look was in his eye again, and then he went on smoothly, so smoothly that she was sure she must have been imagining it, 'So, what do you do when you *do* work?' he asked.

He was pretty sure he knew the answer. It was predictable. She would probably say that she modelled a bit, or flitted from job to job, or dabbled in something to do with the fashion world. Something that gave a thin veneer of respectability to her true career—leeching off rich men.

'It depends what you mean by work,' she countered. She didn't want to talk about her life before she met Stephanos. That era was over now.

'Earning money?' he suggested dryly.

'Oh, that kind of work,' she answered, with deliberate lightness. 'Well, I'm fortunate enough not to have to do that. Especially now, of course. Thanks to Stephanos. He's made everything so much easier.'

It was true. Stephanos's generosity had been fantastic, more than filling the gap left by her coming out to Greece.

Silent white rage filled Nikos. She had the audacity, the sheer, unashamed gall, to sit there and tell him that Stephanos provided all the money she needed—and that even before, when he hadn't, there had been some other man to do so!

'So, life is one long holiday for you, then?' He made himself smile. Forced himself.

Had something of his underlying fury come through? There was a momentary flickering, an uncertain expression in her eyes. She opened her mouth, about to say something, but before she could speak the *maître d'* was gliding up to them, asking whether everything was to their liking.

They nodded their assent, and he bowed and took his leave again, and the moment had gone. It was just as well. She must not get the slightest suspicion of what he felt about her.

He changed the subject, telling her of his itinerary for the following day. A general tour of the island, to get the feel of the place, and then see what was already available, should he wish to buy something immediately. There had been some villas built along the coast, and conversions made of old Venetian merchant houses around the harbour at Skarios Town, or farms and village houses in the interior.

Whether or not he found something he wanted to buy,

he would definitely need something to rent for the next week or two. He wanted Janine Fareham to himself, in his company 24/7. A tucked-away villa would be ideal.

A perfect little love-nest…

He suppressed a mocking smile.

Love wasn't a currency Janine Fareham dealt in.

She wouldn't know the meaning of the word.

CHAPTER THREE

JANINE stood on her balcony, her eyes dreamy. The soft night wind played in her hair; the scent of jasmine and honeysuckle wafted from the gardens below. She should go indoors, she knew, and take off the beautiful dress, and all her make-up, brush out her hair and slip into bed, go to sleep...

And dream of Nikos Kiriakis...dream about every moment she had spent with him.

Confusion filled her. What was he doing to her, making her think about him like this? Making her want to dream about him? Making her want to think about nothing and no one except him.

What was it about Nikos Kiriakis that filled her with yearning like this? Feelings she had never felt before.

Never let herself feel before. Never wanted to feel before.

She'd always been so wary of falling for men—all her life. Always on her guard. She'd grown up watching her mother flit from one affair to another, one man to another, like a butterfly sipping nectar from an endless procession of flowers. At first, at the beginning of every affair, her mother would be ecstatic, devoting herself totally to whoever her latest lover was, and then it would always fall flat, and she would mope and be miserable—until the next man came along.

And there had always been a next man. One had never been enough, whoever he was. She had never looked for commitment, or any kind of permanent relationship—had said it was stifling, claustrophobic. She had always wanted to be free—free to have another affair, and another...

Janine's eyes shadowed. She could not live her life like that. She had more sense.

And the life she'd chosen to lead had made it easy to be sensible about men. Very easy. She'd had other things to occupy her mind.

But now you haven't—and till now you've never met a man like Nikos Kiriakis...

The voice whispered in her ear—enticing, insidious.

The image of his face swam before her eyes.

For a few precious moments she let it linger, luxuriating in delineating every superb feature, recalling every look in his gold-flecked eyes, every smile of that beautiful, sensual mouth.

For once, just for *once*, she wanted to forget everything else, ignore everything else except thinking, *feeling* about the man she could not get out of her head. Who was simply sweeping her away...

She wasn't her mother. Wasn't going to become like her. Hadn't her life so far proved that? Hadn't she followed a completely different path from the one her mother had taken? Surely for once she could indulge in going weak at the knees over a man? A man who took the breath from her body.

She sighed. Oh, yes, falling for Nikos Kiriakis would be so very, very easy.

And totally insane!

Don't do it! Just—don't do it!

She sighed again. And went to bed.

She dreamt of him all night. She tried desperately not to. Kept waking and trying to dream of something else—anything else. Anything! But still he came back in every dream. She could not banish him.

And in the morning, when she finally awoke, she found her heart was filled with a lightness, an eagerness for which there was only one explanation.

She was going to spend the day with Nikos Kiriakis.

And she didn't care that she should want to. The sun was shining down like gold on the world outside, the crimson bougainvillea was vivid on the white, white stone of the buildings, and the blue of the sea and the sky and the pool almost blinded her with their brilliance. Everything seemed brighter, more vivid, more vibrant—and she knew why, and didn't care. Excitement filled her, and anticipation, and her heart skittered, missing little beats as she got herself ready. Ready for Nikos Kiriakis.

Getting dressed took for ever. She discarded at least six outfits. Too casual, too overdressed, too beachy, too stuffy, too revealing, too concealing...

In the end she settled for a short pale green flared skirt and a white tank-top that rode up a fraction over her tummy, but not much. It was sleeveless, but not too décolleté. With it she wore a bead necklace and bangle, and flat, strappy sandals. She pulled her hair back into a long ponytail, clipped on a pair of looped earrings, and stared critically at her reflection.

It would have to do. She put on some lip gloss, a twist of mascara—that was enough. This was a daytime expedition on a holiday island. Anything more by way of make-up would look ridiculous. She grabbed a floppy white sun-hat, her dark glasses and her bag. Then, without looking any further in the mirror, she set off downstairs.

Her heart was beating faster already.

He was waiting for her in the lobby, as they'd agreed the night before. He was casually dressed himself, in polo shirt and chinos, and even though they were obviously designer they gave him a relaxed air. Not that he looked relaxed, she thought suddenly. He'd tensed as she'd approached, and his eyes had narrowed slightly.

Or had they flared?

She could tell. Tell he was reacting to her. Was suddenly excruciatingly self-conscious about it. About herself. The way he was looking at her. The way she wanted to look at him. She had to force herself to keep walking up to him, putting a natural-looking smile on her face.

'Hi,' she said. Her voice sounded breathy.

'*Kalimera,*' said Nikos Kiriakis. His eyes were doing that rapid, totalising flicker over her face, her figure, and she could feel the moment her pulse started to race as he did so. Then his eyes came to rest on hers.

Whoosh! She just about heard the rocket go off in her head.

How could she have forgotten—in the few short hours since her last vivid, oh, so vivid dream of Nikos Kiriakis— just what it was like to have those night-dark gold-flecked eyes looking into hers?

'Are you ready?'

His voice was deep, accented. She wanted him to speak again, to go on speaking, so she could hear that beautiful dark voice talking to her. Wanted to go on staring into those beautiful dark eyes…

'Janine?'

There was no tension in his face now, only a thread of amusement in his voice, as though he well understood her reason for standing there and staring at him like an idiot. She started, and tried to collect herself.

'Yes. Thanks. Um—shall we go?'

A smile tugged at his lips. She tried not to look. Her pulse was shooting all over the place.

She shifted her weight to her other leg and tightened her grip on her shoulder bag.

'Then let us be off.'

He guided her from the hotel. The heat hit her like a hammer the moment she stepped out from the air-conditioned interior into the shaded portico. A car was drawn up, a large, expensive German-marque four-door saloon—obviously the best the hire car company possessed, she surmised. Nikos opened the door for her and she climbed in, sinking down low in the passenger seat, grateful for the air-conditioning which was already taking effect. He crossed around the front of the car and got in on his side, folding his long limbs beside her. Suddenly the car, which had seemed huge, seemed very small.

'Seat belt,' he prompted. Hastily Janine fumbled with the belt and drew it down across her. It seemed to slide very tightly between her breasts, tautening the material of her tank top so that each globe was conspicuously outlined.

She saw his eyes hover on them and dipped her head, feeling flustered, trying to get the buckle of the seat belt into its socket.

'Allow me,' said Nikos, and twisted slightly to complete the task for her.

She yanked her hands away as soon as she could, but not before she felt the touch of his fingers against hers as he guided in the buckle.

It felt like an electric shock.

She buried her hands in her lap, gazing resolutely out through the windscreen as he gunned the engine and eased out of the parking slot. Even more resolutely she did not let her eyes glance down and sideways, to where his hand had curved over the gear lever.

'Where did you want to go first?' she said with determined brightness, as he moved the car forward and down the hotel's driveway towards the road.

She'd gone into hyper-aware mode again; she could tell. It was as if he were radiating some incredibly powerful forcefield that held her motionless in position, all her molecules charged, taken up into a higher energy level. Everything seemed more vivid, more real, than it had ever done before.

He gained the road, swung out onto the right-hand side, and stepped on the accelerator. The powerful car moved forward effortlessly.

'I'm going to follow the coast road south, then drop

down to Lethoni and take a look round there. Then rejoin the road and circle round to Skarios Town. Have you been there yet?'

He turned his head to glance at her, and she felt she needed to give him an answering look.

He'd slid a pair of sunglasses on, and she was grateful. It meant she wasn't exposed to that dark gold-flecked gaze directly. On the other hand, Nikos Kiriakis in a pair of dark glasses took her breath away…

'Er—no. Not yet,' she managed to get out. 'I've not really left the hotel. Stephanos wasn't too keen on me going out and about on my own.'

Nikos felt his mouth tighten. Smart guy, Stephanos. Letting Janine Fareham wander around looking the way she did would be an open invitation to have her snapped up by the first passing predatory male.

Did the girl have any idea what she looked like?

Emotions conflicted within him. She'd sauntered up to him, looking so breathakingly lovely, even in that simple outfit, that he'd felt his whole body respond. Her figure was perfection. Legs not too long, breasts not too slight—not too thin, and certainly not too fat. Some slim girls simply ended up looking like a bag of bones—but not Janine Fareham! There was a softness about her, but a fitness—in both senses of the word!—too. Yet she didn't look like some muscular athletic type. She just looked—

Beautiful. That was the word that kept thumping back into his mind. Beautiful. Nothing more, nothing less. Beautiful.

Natural.

Breathtaking.

Desirable.

Beautiful.

She wasn't wearing any perfume—she knew enough not to wear scent in the sun—yet there was her own scent about her. Shampoo, maybe, or skin cream, or just—just Janine. He wanted to inhale it, breathe it in.

He wanted to taste it...

Taste her.

No! He slammed a lid down on his reaction.

Not yet. He might want Janine Fareham, want to feel that soft body in his arms, want to feel her breasts tighten against him, want to taste that sweet, honeyed mouth, taste all of her, every inch—but not yet. He had to play this carefully. Very carefully. If he came on to her too strong she might get nervous.

Worse than nervous.

Suspicious.

She seemed to have swallowed it whole, that Stephanos had asked him to look after her...

Theos! He smothered a savage laugh. What lover in his right sense would send another man to look after his mistress? Let alone a man with the kind of reputation that Nikos enjoyed in Athens!

Yet she had believed it. Believed him.

A slight frown threatened between his eyes. As before— yesterday, in the sea—he felt a thread of reluctance take shape within him. Reluctance to do to Janine Fareham what he knew he was going to do. What he had to do.

As before, he put it aside. It didn't matter that he was deceiving her, was following his own private agenda with her. She was threatening his sister—his sister who had enough troubles in her life without the added anguish of a husband besotted with another woman.

A woman any man could so easily become besotted with...

His eyes narrowed.

Well, not him. Definitely not him.

He was here to do a job. Complete a task. Help his sister.

His expression lightened again. He did not need to feel any compunction about what he was going to do. Janine

Fareham had made a mistake when she'd selected his brother-in-law for her next protector. His face hardened when he thought of the damage she was so thoughtlessly doing by having this affair with Stephanos. No, he told himself reassuringly, he did not need to feel anything for the girl except desire. And it wasn't, he went on, as if she wouldn't get a great deal of pleasure from what he intended for her. He knew he would.

That sense of satisfaction filled him again. He was here to seduce Janine Fareham, save his sister's marriage, and, into the bargain, have a very enjoyable brief affair with a very lovely woman. How could he feel bad about that?

He revved the engine, changed gear with a fast, fluent movement, and stepped on the accelerator, pulling out sharply. Two seconds later the camper van that had been slowing him down was far behind.

Janine smothered a sharp gasp of fear. Nikos had pulled out to overtake so abruptly she hadn't realised what he intended, and for a second she had been staring out of the windscreen on the wrong side of the road, with a blind corner coming up in what had seemed nothing more than a handful of yards ahead. Then, just as abruptly, Nikos had swung the car back onto the right side of the road, and taken the corner in a smooth, powerful movement.

Her nails, she discovered, were digging into the palms of her hands, and her spine ached from where she'd had to exert all her muscles not to sway precipitously.

He turned to her and grinned as he sped the car up the ascending slope of the road towards yet another hairpin. Thankfully, this time there were no other cars in the way for him to overtake.

'Frightened I'll crash?' he asked, his mouth tugging back.

She felt her heart crunch again as she took in the full impact of his smile.

'You wouldn't like to slow down a bit, would you?' she asked faintly.

His grin deepened. He changed gear again, glancing briefly back at the road, then at her again, and then finally—thankfully—the road, curling around the next hairpin in a tight, engine-revving manoeuvre.

'I've never had an accident yet,' he assured her, 'and I don't intend to.'

No, she thought, he wouldn't crash. Nikos Kiriakis would speed through life, foot down on the accelerator, and other cars—everything else—would get out of his way. He was a man who would get where he wanted. Get what he wanted.

Especially women.

She bit her lip. When Nikos Kiriakis wanted a woman he'd just go and get her. Help himself.

And what woman would say no?

What woman in their right mind would say no?

Would I? Would I say no?

A warm, shivery languor stole through her. In her mind's eye she saw herself, saw Nikos Kiriakis walking up to her, purpose in his eye, walking up to her and taking her hand, leading her to his bed and helping himself to her. Making her his own...

She felt the warmth of her blood, felt the soft, persistent vibration of the car beneath her thighs, felt her breath quicken. The vision seemed so real, the fantasy so tangible, she could hardly believe it existed only in her own imagination.

The fantasy of Nikos Kiriakis helping himself to her. Would she say no? *Could* she say no?

The question teased at her. The answer crushed her.

He hasn't asked you yet...and what makes you think he's going to?

She risked another glance at him.

In profile he was even more fantastic than full-on—if that were possible. His cheekbones were high, his nose strong and straight, his jaw clearly defined. And then there was that mouth—so beautifully sculpted.

She had a sudden vivid vision of that mouth moving over her skin…

Determinedly she dragged her gaze away, and looked out over the countryside instead.

That was what she must focus on. Nikos Kiriakis might be looking for a villa, but she—she was looking for Greece. At Greece.

Stephanos's country.

And now hers. Thanks to Stephanos, who had brought her here. To his home.

That was to be her home now.

A strangeness went through her. Her eyes stole back to Nikos Kiriakis. His land too. His home. His country.

All around—from islands to mountains, from seas to forests—this ancient, timeless country was his. The country that had been the cradle of western civilisation, whose art and thought still illuminated the world, twenty-five centuries later.

She looked around her. The ancient landscape was bathed in the light of the sun, unchanged, it seemed to her, for thousands of years. The olive groves, trees with their clusters of ripening fruits, their silvery leaves so carefully pruned and tended. A tethered donkey, grazing in the shade of a tree. Vineyards, low and lush, and, where there was space, the dark splash of purple on the ground, where rich grapes spread out to dry into sweet raisins.

As he drove the expensive, powerful car along this road, which wound and meandered as it had done for centuries, even when nothing more than an unmetalled track, she watched him. They closed in on a tractor drawing a cart. She could see the back of the farmer driving it. Nikos slowed down. Unlike the camper van, he did not pass it immediately, did not roar past in his expensive car. Instead he waited patiently, until the tractor turned off into a field, before speeding up. It was a small gesture, but illuminating.

She found it reassuring.

They had climbed over a spur of the land as it headed down towards the most southerly promontory of the island. The hairpins were done now, and Janine felt herself relax more as they cruised through this fertile landscape.

'What are those trees?' she asked. 'They're not olives.'

'Citrus. Orange or lemon,' he answered. 'The Ionian islands are very fertile—even Skarios, though it is further south than the others, and drier. Historically, their main importance was strategic—they were coveted by the Venetians, who ruled the islands on and off, and then later the British, of course. Now their main contribution is tourism. Some would say they have been over-developed, especially Corfu, though it is still perfectly possible to find quieter parts away from the resorts. But that is why there is such concern that Skarios should be developed carefully, without repeating the mistakes made on other islands.'

She gazed around. 'It's so beautiful as it is—the last thing you'd want is high-rise resorts and so on.'

He nodded. 'Stephanos has got it right with his hotel here—it melds into the natural landscape. He will, I hope, have considerable influence on what happens to the island.'

She glanced at him. 'Do you really want to buy a villa here?'

He was silent a moment. 'If I find something suitable,' he said at last. 'But I want to get a feel for the place first. The turning for Lethoni is just coming up—its main claim to fame is the Venetian fortress.'

She frowned. 'What were the Venetians doing in Greece?' she asked.

'Conquering it,' he answered dryly, swinging the car off the main coast road and down towards the promontory on which the little town of Lethoni sat, dominated by its Venetian fort. 'Greece is a crossroads,' he went on. 'Not wealthy in its own right—we are still a relatively poor country for Europe—but useful. The Venetians coming from the west, like the Ottoman Turks coming from the East, coveted the riches of the Byzantine empire. Greece— just got in the way.'

They wound down the narrow road into the small village, dwarfed by its huge stone fortress, standing four-square against all comers, by land or sea. There was a shingly beach beside the fortress, and some shops and restaurants and bars, and some old seventeenth-century Venetian houses, looking slightly strange here, with their Italianate style of archicture. Nikos parked the car and they got out. Again, the heat hit like a furnace.

Janine stood staring at the dark mass of the fortress, bag over her shoulder, sunhat in her hand. Nikos came round to her.

'The day is heating. You must put your hat on or you will burn.'

Without asking he took the hat from her suddenly nerveless fingers and placed it on her head, smoothing away loose strands of hair. He smiled down at her.

'There,' he said. His hands slid to her shoulders, resting there a moment. 'Now you are protected.'

Protected? The word mocked in her brain. She stood there, quite motionless, while Nikos Kiriakis rested his hands on her shoulders and smiled down at her. His hands were warm on her skin, closing over the curves of her shoulders, where her bare arms met the tank top she was wearing. His thumbs brushed close to her throat.

She felt as if every nerve in her body were firing at once. Simultaneously.

Her lips parted, eyes hanging helplessly on his, even though she could not see them, even though the black, glittering surface of his dark lenses looked down at her unreadably.

Protected? She had never felt less protected in her life. Never in more danger!

He dropped his hands away.

'Would you like to have a coffee? The bar over there seems pleasant enough.'

He pointed to where a café sat, by the edge of the little beach on which some local children were playing, and they wandered across, taking a table in the shade of a large striped awning. Janine gazed across the beach to the fortress beyond.

'Can one go round it?' she asked, for something to say—something to try and sound normal.

Nikos said something in Greek to the waiter who had come out to take their orders. Then he turned back to Janine.

'Apparently it is closed, awaiting renovation. Parts of it are in such disrepair it is dangerous. In the early years of the last century it was used as a prison. The plan now is to open it as a tourist attraction, possibly using the main courtyard as a concert venue. But nothing has yet been decided for certain. As you can see—' he gestured around '—this is a sleepy place.'

Janine followed Nikos's gaze. On closer inspection the buildings, though pretty, were peeling, and one or two obviously were closed up, with boarded windows.

'It could be lovely!' she exclaimed.

'Indeed, yes. But it must be carefully done. One of my interests here, apart from searching for a villa for myself, is to see what investment can be made to restore such places as Lethoni.'

He gave the order for coffee, watched the waiter depart, then turned back to Janine.

'It's an interest I have in many such communities across Greece. Investments must be carefully made, so that any restoration or development is in keeping with the traditional style and way of life. The idea is to revive communities so that they may thrive once more in a new economy. In rural or remote areas, such as here, too many people have to leave to seek employment in larger centres. Only the old people are left. But there is also a danger that too much development will not only ruin these places, but also attract entrepreneurs from the cities, who simply arrive to take over any opportunities for profit from local people, who are left out of the loop.'

She looked troubled. 'Is that what Stephanos is doing?' She did not like to think of him profiting from this beautiful island at the expense of the islanders.

Nikos gave a wry smile. 'On the contrary. His hotel is a joint venture with Skariot business partners, plus all the staff are local, and a good percentage of the profits will be reinvested in the island's infrastructure. Stephanos owns hotels all over the world, but those in Greece are very special to him.'

She smiled. 'I'm glad. He's such a lovely man—he doesn't seem like a ruthless businessman at all!'

Nikos's smile became yet more wry. 'He can be very tough, when necessary, in business. I learnt a lot from him!'

Her eyes widened. 'You? But you seem loads tougher than Stephanos! He's such a total pussycat!'

'To you he is indulgent,' responded Nikos. She would have had to be deaf not to hear the cynical note in his voice.

Her chin lifted. 'Is it so surprising? In the circumstances?'

Again, as she had last night over dinner, she felt a sudden frisson of unease go through her.

If Lethoni was so sleepy it seemed to be in permanent siesta, Skarios Town, the main town on the island, was by contrast a hive of bustling activity. Though it wasn't unbearably crowded, it was certainly busy, with a good proportion of shops dedicated to the influx of holidaymakers who had already discovered this off-the-beaten-track island.

Janine sat dutifully while Nikos made clear his requirements to the town's two estate agents. The entire conversation was in Greek, obviously, and though Janine glanced curiously at some of the details of villas which were presented with great deference to their clearly very wealthy prospective client, only the pictures made sense, not the Greek writing. For the most part she simply sat and watched Nikos.

It was a joy simply to be able to watch him while he was busy doing something else. It was incredible, she found herself thinking in amazement. She had seen good-looking men before—they had been no strangers to her when she was growing up with her mother, in her rootless, purposeless existence—yet no one had ever had the kind of impact this man was having on her now.

It was everything about him—not just his looks, but the way he talked, moved. The way his hand slashed when he didn't like something; the way his palm opened expansively when he did. The way he held his head, with that slightly arrogant tilt to it, and the way he talked, even though she could not understand what he said, that spoke of a man who knew exactly what he wanted and expected to get it.

And was *she* on that list of things he wanted and expected to get?

He folded the last of the presentations away and got to his feet, drawing out one of the sets of details. Presumably, thought Janine, as she got to her feet too, one of them had found possible favour.

'Anything interesting?' she asked, as they walked out onto the cobbled street.

He gave a shrug. 'Possibly. But I took this to be polite more than anything.' He indicated the brochure he'd been given. He changed the subject. 'Now, you are a woman, and here are some shops—time for some retail therapy! As for me, I shall suffer in silence—and simply be on hand to do my masculine duty and pay for everything!'

There was resigned humour in his voice, as though he knew indeed that it was his lot in life to pay for what women purchased.

She gave an outraged laugh. 'You will not!' she exclaimed. 'I'll buy my own souvenirs, thank you! You don't have to pay for me.'

He glanced at her. 'I thought that was Stephanos's privilege,' he said dryly.

Her face stiffened suddenly. 'I do have money of my own,' she answered. 'Stephanos has been incredibly generous, yes—how could I possibly deny that?—but I'm not dependent on him.'

'No?' The doubt in his voice made her feel uncomfortable.

'No,' she answered firmly. 'And I'm not dependent on you, Mr Kiriakis, to buy my souvenirs!'

'Nikos.' He took her arm, his hand closing over her flesh, stopping her in the street. 'My name is Nikos.'

He was looking down at her. Too close. She could not see his expression, could not see his eyes, but she felt her heart suddenly give a little thrill.

'Nikos,' he repeated softly, and then with humour in his voice, real humour now, he let her go. 'And you may, with my blessing, buy all your own souvenirs!'

Her heart gave another little thrill—for a quite different reason this time. Nikos Kiriakis amused was just as capable of sending her heart-rate haywire as Nikos being formidable!

In the end she only bought one souvenir, a pretty little embroidered pouch that she could keep jewellery in. She paid for it herself.

'Is that all?' Nikos frowned.

She nodded.

Was that her appeal? he found himself thinking cynically. That she was cheap to run? Even as he framed the question he mocked it. Oh, no. Janine Fareham had an appeal that was nothing, absolutely nothing to do with whether she was cheap to keep or not!

He watched her walk out of the shop ahead of him. The flared skirt was made of soft material, and moulded enticingly around the roundness of her bottom. Drawing his eyes to it.

And not his alone. He was not the only male present to be aware, very aware, of her blonde beauty. He intercepted one tourist looking lustingly after her, and found himself glaring at him aggressively. The man got the message and flicked his eyes away hurriedly.

Nikos followed Janine out of the shop. He did not like other men looking at her like that. He closed up on her. Without thinking about it, he realised he was reaching his arm to drape it around her shoulder and draw her closer to him.

Her head twisted, eyes flaring to his, and he could distinctly feel her tense under the hand that was over the curve of her shoulder.

He smiled down at her.

'Lunch?' he suggested. 'Let's try down by the harbour.'

For a moment she just stayed frozen. He wished he could see her eyes, but she'd replaced her dark glasses in the glare of the sun. But he didn't need to see her pupils to know that they were flaring.

Satisfaction went through him. He liked the idea of Janine Fareham responding to him. He liked it a lot.

He walked her down to the harbour, his arm still around her shoulder. He told himself it was to keep other tourists at bay, both physically and visually, as they threaded through the crowded narrow street. That it was part of his careful campaign to move in on her, stage by stage, until he could make his final move on her.

But there was another reason, too, he knew, why he kept his arm around her.

Because it felt good. It felt the right place for his arm to be.

And because Janine Fareham felt good pulled against him, very good. Very good indeed.

'Red or blue?'

His voice was genial as he indicated, with his free hand, the two restaurants with seating areas across the roadway right beside the harbour. One had a red awning covering the tables, the other a blue.

'I don't mind.'

Was there something a little odd about her voice? he wondered. A little strained?

He smiled. 'What is it you say in English, when you are trying to choose? *Any, many, many more*?'

Janine gave a laugh. It helped to break the strain that had engulfed her ever since Nikos had walked out of the souvenir shop and casually, as if it was the most obvious thing in the world to do, put his arm around her.

Her stomach had dropped to the ground and her heart-rate had gone crazy! For a moment she had simply stalled, unable to do anything except register the 'whoosh' that had gone off inside her again. Then, frantically, she'd tried to regain control of her reactions. She mustn't make anything out of what he'd done. It had been a casual gesture on his part, to guide her through the crowds. Nothing more!

'It's *eeny-meeny-miny-mo*,' she corrected him. 'And, no, I haven't the faintest idea what it means. Um—how about that one?' She pointed to the restaurant with the blue awning. 'There's a table free right by the water's edge.'

They made their way over to it, the shade of the awning taking away some of the heat. Janine sat down, slipped off her sunglasses and scraped off her sunhat, then untied her hair and shook it loose with a feeling of relief. As her head stilled she realised Nikos was looking at her.

He'd taken his dark glasses off at last, and she reeled under the full impact of his power-on gaze.

Weakness washed down through her. She could feel her lips parting wordlessly, her pupils dilating. Colour flaring along her cheekbones.

Then abruptly, like a light turned off, the moment ended. Nikos had turned his head as the waiter approached, placing menus down on the table and hovering attentively.

Janine reached fumblingly for one of the menus, but as she stared at it uncomprehendingly it was not only because she was staring at the Greek pages. It was because she was completely incapable of thinking.

Desire. Naked, blatant desire. That was what she'd seen in those intense gold-flecked eyes. Nothing more and, dear God alive, nothing less!

As if reaching for a shield she fumbled on the table surface, lighting on her dark glasses, and shoved them back on her nose as quickly as her trembling hands could manage. Then and only then did she feel safe. Safe enough to answer Nikos's enquiry as to what she would like to drink.

Her breathing felt ragged, and yet she managed to get out, 'Oh, just mineral water, please—sparkling,' before taking refuge once again in the menu. After another moment she realised she was still looking at the Greek pages, and hurriedly turned over to the pages which repeated the menu in both English and German, for the tourists.

Slowly she got control back over her body.

With real effort of mind, she focused on the menu.

'I think I'll just have a Greek salad,' she said at last. 'I can't face anything hot in this heat!'

'You're not tempted by the squid, then?' Nikos's voice was lightly baiting.

That powerful intensity had gone from his eyes, his face. It made it easier. Easier for her to try and be normal. She pulled an expression of exaggerated disgust.

'No sale! Not while they have wiggly tentacles with suckers on them!'

Nikos laughed. 'Fried in batter, you don't see the suckers.'

She waved her hands in horrified negation and he laughed again, then gave his order to the hovering waiter. Janine listened to the rapid Greek and caught not a word. She sighed. It was a tough language to learn. She couldn't even read a menu unless it was translated.

I'm going to have to try and learn, she thought. For Stephanos's sake.

The waiter took his leave, scurrying away, and Nikos's gaze came back to Janine.

He found his eyes softening. That moment, just now, when she'd shaken her hair loose, revealing her eyes from behind those shades, had kicked him—hard. The combination of that fabulous golden hair tumbling over her near naked shoulders and those beautiful chestnut eyes had riveted him. And when he'd seen her lips part, her pupils dilate like that as he'd looked at her, then it had been even more potent.

She'd been helpless, it was obvious. Helpless to do anything except let him look at her. She couldn't fight it, couldn't deny it. She'd just had to sit there and let him make it very, very clear to her just what he felt about her.

Now he wanted to reach out and touch her, stroke her bare arm as it lay on the blue and white paper tablecloth, close his hand over hers, wind his fingers with hers…

A strange feeling went through him. Desire, yes, but something more. He wanted to touch her, but not with desire, not just now. Now he just wanted to touch her…well, because. That was all. Because he did. Just as he'd wanted to put his arm around her as they'd left the souvenir shop.

To show her, and all the world, that she was his.

His body stilled. How could he be feeling possessive about Janine Fareham? He couldn't care less about her! He simply needed to remove her from Stephanos, get her out of his sister's marriage!

His mouth tightened. There was nothing *personal* about what he was doing. Janine Fareham was simply an obstacle, an impediment, a problem that had to be neutralised.

He'd better make sure he remembered that.

'Seen enough?'

Nikos's voice was lazy and amused. Janine turned round and felt her heart give that familiar skip it gave every time she set eyes on him again. He was leaning against a half-ruined wall, arms crossed, looking very relaxed.

He also looked quite untroubled by the afternoon heat, which even in this elevated position, which caught what little breeze there was, was still punishing. For herself, she felt hot and sticky, her feet chalky with dust. But Nikos Kiriakis just went on looking cool—in both senses of the word.

'Just about,' she answered. 'Sorry to have spent so long,' she went on, as she threaded her way towards him carefully amongst the broken masonry. 'But I've never seen a Greek temple before.'

'Never?' Nikos's voice was mildly enquiring.

'I've never been to Greece before,' she explained.

Was there something strange about her voice? he wondered. If so, he could not imagine why there should be.

Then she was speaking again. 'It's not really my end of the Med.'

'Spain?'

She shook her head, negotiating a tricky step.

'The South of France, more.'

Nikos's mouth thinned fractionally. The Côte d'Azur— the glittering French Riviera—oozing money and wealth and rich living. The traditional stamping ground of the adventuress. He was not surprised she was familiar with it.

She had paused by the broken base of a column, gazing around. It was, conceded Nikos, a beautiful place for a temple. He'd spotted the brown archaeological site notice along the road back from the northern extremity of the island, where they'd headed after lunch, and suggested a brief diversion. There wasn't a great deal left of the temple—much of the stone had been taken away over the centuries to build houses—but the views down to the sea were still spectacular. It was a high and lonely place. Just right for communing with the gods.

He'd been surprised at her interest. The site had been open, with no entrance ticket required, but the tourist authorities had set up explanatory noticeboards describing the site and mapping it out as it must once have stood. Janine had pored over them.

She must have spent a good twenty minutes trawling over the site. She seemed excessively taken with it. Nikos had left her to it. There were no other visitors at that time of day, and they were well off the beaten track. He'd watched her wandering around. She had an extraordinary natural grace, he'd found himself thinking—there was great pleasure in watching her.

She didn't look in the least what she was, he realised. He had called her a foxy piece last night, to remind himself just what kind of female she was. He frowned. But the description didn't fit. She was simply beautiful; that was all. With a natural, unforced loveliness in every line of her body, every turn of her head. And her behaviour was not that of a gold-digging mistress either. She'd cast out no lures to him—other than her own natural beauty!—made no attempt to flirt with him or attract him. Oh, she was highly self-conscious of him, that much was obvious, but there had been no deliberate come-on from her—nor any deliberate invitation.

His frown deepened. He should not be surprised that it had taken an exceptional woman to snare Stephanos away from his wife. As a rich man, Stephanos had all his life been pursued by women, just as he was himself. As Nikos was doing now, so Stephanos had enjoyed a good selection of them when he was younger. Then, of course, he had fallen in love with Demetria, and from then on no other woman had existed for him. He'd laid siege to her, determined to wait it out until she found the courage to divorce her first husband.

Nikos's eyes flickered. Love was a quite alien concept to him. He could not imagine falling in love with a woman. Desiring her, yes. But not loving her. As for going to any lengths to win her—well, that was beyond him as well. Yet not Stephanos, apparently. Stephanos had endured the wrath of his beloved's father, who hadn't wanted his daughter's marriage overturned, had stood by her when she did finally find the courage to end her marriage, and had married her the moment she was legally free to do so.

That was devotion indeed!

Nikos's mouth tightened. And yet it looked as if he was risking all that for a hole-and-corner adulterous affair with a twenty-five-year-old girl!

He watched her now, as she took a careful step down the ancient stairs. As her weight shifted, suddenly the cracked paving wobbled precariously. He was there in an instant, hands closing around her slender waist, steadying her.

For a moment, timeless and motionless, he felt her soft body pliant in his arms, her breasts crushed against his chest. Then, slowly, he lowered her to the ground and eased back from her, still touching her waist with his hands.

'OK?' he asked.

Janine caught her breath. Her heart was skidding away.

'Fine. Yes. Thanks.' Her answer was totally distracted. She could do nothing except gaze helplessly up at him.

His hands fell away from her waist. Immediately she felt bereft.

He smiled down at her.

'Time to go?'

She followed meekly after him, back to the little car park

down an unmade track from the road. She fought hard to regain her composure.

Nikos, however, she realised, was totally relaxed. Had it meant nothing to him, then, that unintentional embrace? Her eyes flickered to him as he drove off. Sexy as those dark glasses were, they were very frustrating. She could not see his eyes, or tell their expression.

His thoughts were veiled from her.

Hers, however, were all too transparent.

CHAPTER FOUR

THE silky water of the swimming pool slid over Janine's body, soothing the ragged edges of her mind. Her thoughts were going round and round in her head. Had been doing so ever since that moment in the temple.

Now, as she glided slowly up and down the pool in the early evening, she tried to confront them.

She was in danger, serious danger, of falling for a man it would be madness to fall for under any circumstances. Let alone these. She was here in Greece for Stephanos, that was all! For no other reason. There was no room in her life for falling for a man like Nikos. Outside Greece her life was so completely different from what Stephanos had given her—and here in Greece her focus had to be Stephanos. It had to be! Nikos Kiriakis was a complication she could do without.

A dangerous complication.

She did a sudden dive, as if she could escape her thoughts.

She surfaced in a shower of water drops and took a lungful of air, reaching with her toes for the bottom of the pool, which was just in her depth still.

Across on the other side, she saw that one of the male hotel guests was playing with his children in the pool, while his wife sunned herself. He punched an inflatable ball through the air and his children plunged after it like a school of baby dolphins, squealing delightedly. He looked after them, smiling broadly.

Something gave Janine a pang. One of the children, a little girl about ten years old, she thought, came paddling triumphantly back to her father, pushing the ball in front of her and calling out in a soft, piping Greek voice, *'Vava, Vava!'*—Papa! Papa!

The man held out his arms to his daughter.

'Ela!'

It was a word Janine had become familiar with. She wasn't sure what it meant, but the parents here often used it to respond to their children's calls. She watched the little girl swim up to her father, present him with the ball, and wrap him in a big hug. He laughed, and kissed her wet hair affectionately before tossing the ball to his other children.

Lucky little girl.

The words were in Janine's mind before she could stop them.

Lucky little girl to have a father to play with her, dote on her...

She had not been so fortunate.

She'd sometimes wondered if her mother even *knew* who had fathered her. She'd been so evasive, so completely indifferent all Janine's childhood, that she'd given up trying to find out. When she was a teenager she'd realised just how impossible it was for a woman to tell who had fathered her child if she slept with more than one man during a menstrual cycle. So perhaps her mother simply didn't know, she'd concluded chillingly.

She hadn't even had any clues from her own appearance. She was blonde, just like her mother, and apart from her chestnut-coloured eyes, physically very similar. So much so that as her mother had gotten older it had become obvious that she found it increasingly painful to have a grown up daughter hanging around, like a younger version of herself. The self that her mother's unforgiving mirror no longer showed.

It had been a kindness to her mother when Janine had taken herself off—and a relief to herself to be away from the world her mother adored, making a new life for herself. She hadn't missed the world she'd grown up in—the endless partying, the obsession with appearance, her mother's constant need to have men around her. It was all so superficial, so pointless, so purposeless. That was why she'd made her own life so different.

But it had still been a shock when she'd heard of her mother's death three years ago, even if she *had* died the way she'd lived. In a smashed-up sports car with another woman's husband in the driving seat. The post-mortems had shown that both of them were well over the limit for alcohol.

With her mother gone she'd had no other relatives in the world, so far as she knew. No one to whom she meant anything more than friendship.

Her face shadowed. Then Stephanos had come, like a gift from heaven, into her life. Her gratitude to him was boundless. She would make the very most of him she could, however little that could be.

As for Nikos Kiriakis, she wouldn't think about him.

He was dangerous. And he was unnecessary.

And she was better off without him.

Nikos strolled out onto his balcony. The setting sun streamed over the gardens, silhouetting the slender pointed cypress trees that framed the vista. Stephanos had chosen well, he thought. The site was superb. And his architects had done him proud. He had selected the best.

A frown furrowed between his eyes. Down in the pool he could see Janine, swimming slowly up and down.

He'd selected the best for his mistress, too. The day he'd just spend with Janine Fareham had made him realise just what it was about her that so beguiled his brother-in-law. It wasn't just her beauty, outstanding though that was. It was the way she moved, the way she smiled and laughed, the way she brushed her hair back off her face—every gesture caught at him. Captivated him.

He stilled. That was a dangerous word—captivated.

He put it aside. It had no place in what he wanted of the girl who was causing his sister so much anguish.

All I have to do is take her to bed. Nothing else.

That, surely, he thought with cynical self-mockery, would not be too hard a task! He only had to think of Janine to want her.

Deliberately he recalled the way she'd felt in his arms as he'd caught her in that ruined temple. Her body had felt so soft, so rounded, so enticing. He'd been hardening against her when he'd put her away from him.

And so had she. He had felt her breasts swelling against him.

It had been intoxicating.

Captivating…

His mouth thinned. What was wrong with him? Janine Fareham was a beauty, and he enjoyed taking beautiful women to bed. They enjoyed it too. He saw to that. He didn't have to be captivated by them to bed them!

And he certainly wasn't about to be captivated by the likes of Stephanos's young mistress. On the contrary, it was *she* who was going to be captivated by *him*. And he was making good progress on that score, he knew. Throughout the day her response to him had been growing—he'd seen to that, cultivated it carefully, step by step—and that final episode in the temple, when she'd pressed against him, had been the most expressive yet.

The way she'd gazed up at him as he'd held her in his arms. Her lips had been parted, her eyes wide…

Captivating. Quite captivating…

With a jerk of impatience with himself he pulled away from the balcony, striding indoors.

He headed for the phone. Time for stage two in his programme of seduction.

Stage one had been to cultivate Janine Fareham, make her responsive to him. Arouse her appetite.

Stage two was to starve it.

*   *   *

Janine sat at her breakfast table and crumbled tiny pieces of bread for the sparrows that hopped around on the paved terrace, eager for their breakfast too. She fed them in a desultory fashion, but her real attention was focused on looking out for Nikos Kiriakis.

She knew she was, and knew she should not be, but she couldn't help it. She wanted to see him.

She hadn't seen him since he'd dropped her off in the hotel portico the day before and told her he had some phone calls to make. She'd told herself she was glad he hadn't joined her in the pool, that she had no intention of spending any more time with him—no intention of letting him come anywhere near her again—but if that was so then why had she waited in her room until the last possible moment before the buffet stopped serving, just in case he might phone through to her and suggest they dine together again?

And why was she now watching everyone who came and went, longing for each one to be Nikos Kiriakis?

And why was there a dull churning in her stomach as she waited and watched for him though he never came?

A thought struck her like a knife. Had he gone? Left the hotel?

Dismay plunged through her. Dismay at the thought of never seeing Nikos Kiriakis again.

She scraped her chair back abruptly and stood up.

This was bad. She had to stop this. Now. She had to put a lid on this ridiculous reaction she was having. She had to get a grip. Control herself.

Determinedly, she picked up her book and her bag and headed indoors, up to her room. She would keep herself busy today. Take her mind off Nikos Kiriakis. Stop herself recalling in Technicolor detail every last minute of yesterday, and the night before over dinner.

I'll do the windsurfing course, she thought decisively.

Trying to stop myself falling in the water should take my mind off Nikos Kiriakis!

Immediately, like a traitor, came a vivid memory of how he'd moved the salt cellar and cutlery into position with those beautiful long fingers of his, to show her the effects of wind direction on board direction...

She pushed it aside and walked up to Reception to book herself on the course.

She saw him at once, her eyes flying to him, heart leaping like a traitor. He was standing, his back to her, talking to one of the reception desk staff, and he was wearing a hand-tailored business suit again. He looked tall, and dark, and devastating. Her heart leapt again, and then plunged. He had a black leather briefcase on the floor beside him, and she could see car keys in his hand. He said something to the receptionist, who smiled and nodded, and then picked up his briefcase.

He saw her the moment he turned. She was poised, im-mobile, just past the double doors that opened onto the re-ception area. He walked towards her with his lithe, rapid stride.

'Good morning. You look ready for the sun.' His voice was pleasant, his manner amiable. And there was nothing in it, nothing at all, to indicate that to him she was anything more than a woman he had babysat yesterday for the sake of his business associate and friend Stephanos Ephandrou.

She gave an uncertain smile in return, hiding the con-striction in her throat that had suddenly tightened. 'You look ready for work,' she countered.

He gave a wry smile back. 'As you can see. I have sev-eral business appointments today, one of which is in Patra, on the mainland. And what have you planned for today?'

There was no suggestion that she might accompany him. She took her cue, fighting the wave of desolation that was sweeping through her.

'Oh,' she answered brightly—too brightly, 'I've decided

I'm going to give the windsurfing a go. I'm just going to see if there are any lessons free this morning.' She nodded towards the reception desk.

He smiled. 'Very energetic.' He shot the cuff back on his sleeve and glanced at his watch. 'Well, do please excuse me. I must set off.'

'Yes. Of course. Please don't let me keep you.' She kept her composure with iron nerve. Then suddenly, as his body language told her he was about to turn away, she said, 'Thank you so much for taking me out and about yesterday, Mr Kiriakis—'

He stilled. Then, with the slightest pull of his mouth, he replied, 'Nikos.' His voice dropped. 'Nikos,' he repeated. His voice was low, his lashes sweeping down over his cheeks. Briefly, so briefly she thought she must have imagined it, he touched the backs of his fingertips to her cheek.

'Enjoy your windsurfing…'

He smiled, and walked away.

Her eyes followed him all the way out of the hotel, her heart beating like a hammer.

Despite her windsurfing lesson, the day seemed to last for ever. So did the evening. A restlessness filled her, making every minute seem an hour, every hour a tedious eternity. And the windsurfing had left her with muscles aching in unaccustomed places and a severe loss of dignity—she had, as she had known she would, fallen a depressing number of times.

For the rest of the over-long day, the rest of the lonely, tedious evening, she idled the time away fretfully. Whereas she had once revelled in the laziness of being pampered at a five star hotel, now she was discontented. Restless.

Would she ever see Nikos again?

Stop it! she told herself fiercely, over and over again. Be glad he's gone. Grateful. He was the last thing you needed.

But Nikos had done something to her, and it could not

be undone. He had woken something in her that had never been woken before. And it was alive in her—and hungry.

Hungry for him.

She couldn't get Nikos Kiriakis out of her mind. Her thoughts. Her skin. She knew she was being a fool, an idiot—but she couldn't help herself. Endless arguments went round and round in her head as she paraded every reason, every *good* reason, why she should put Nikos Kiriakis out of her mind. And not one of them had the slightest effect on her.

She wanted him.

It was so very, very simple. She wanted him. Wanted to see him, hear him, be near him, feast her eyes on him. Wanted to be in his company, wanted to feel that wonderful, heady sense of intoxication that fired through her whenever she thought of him, remembered him. Remembered those beautiful, dark gold-flecked eyes, that sculpted mouth, the way his silky black hair made her yearn to play her fingers through it, smooth along those high-planed cheekbones, edge along the line of his jaw...

And above all—above all she wanted him to want her—to desire her, to make love to her.

Nikos. Nikos Kiriakis...

His name sang in her head, in her blood. Heating it like a fever. Filling her with a wanting that left her weak, sick.

Please let me see him again—please!

The litany sounded in her head. Relentless. Hopeless.

The next day was even worse. She couldn't face breakfast downstairs, couldn't face another windsurfing lesson. Couldn't face anything. She wanted to be brave and ask Reception if Nikos Kiriakis had checked out, but she didn't dare. Didn't dare admit to herself that if he had she would be desolate.

She tried to think about Stephanos. Think about where he was right now, what time it would be in New York, what he was likely to be doing. She wished she could phone him, speak to him, make him real for her again. To remind her why she was here in Greece. Not to ache for a man who had set her blood on fire but to make the most, the very most, of what she had been given so unexpectedly, so miraculously. Stephanos. Not Nikos. Stephanos.

But it was Nikos she wanted. Nikos she craved.

And Nikos she did not have.

He'd gone. He had to have gone. There was no point hoping otherwise. He must have left, and that was that. Why bother to leave a message for her? He'd done what Stephanos had asked him to do and then got on with his own life.

He'd have a woman somewhere, anyway, in his life. Of course he would! Someone poised and sophisticated and mega-glamorous. A man like that would never be on his own for a second!

Her heart churned as she thought of Nikos Kiriakis with that faceless, poised, sophisticated, mega-glamorous woman at his side. In his arms. His bed.

No! She pushed the tormenting thought aside, shifting restlessly on her lounger beside the pool.

Someone hunkered down beside her.

'So,' said Nikos Kiriakis, 'what happened to the wind-surfing?'

As her eyes flew open, as she heard his voice, her face lit like the dazzle of sunshine after rain. For a second Nikos reeled. Something shot through him, he didn't know what. Then he got his sense back.

Her response was just what he wanted. Confirming that he'd played his hand in exactly the right manner. Whetted her appetite for him—then withdrawn from the scene. Letting her hunger for him.

And she was hungry all right. He saw it leap in her eyes, in the way they lit up, her gaze fastening on his as though she could hardly believe it. He let her gaze feast greedily on him—all of him. Her eyes moved down from his face, widening as they skimmed down over his naked torso, and lower still. The squat he was in made his quads stand out, his forearms resting on them for balance. For a moment he let her go on gazing at him, then he straightened.

'Windsurfing,' he said. 'Let's see what you can do.' He held his hand down to her commandingly.

She took it like a lamb, getting up off the lounger. He frowned. 'You'll need a T-shirt—you'll burn on the water otherwise.'

Wordlessly she groped in her beachbag and drew out a loose white top. For his part he flicked out the dark blue T-shirt he'd had draped over one shoulder and put it on. She did likewise with hers.

He stood in front of her, smiling down at her.

'Ready?'

She nodded, still wordless. Incapable of speech. He took her hand, and they headed down to the windsurf station.

Bliss, thought Janine, her head a haze of delight. Bliss— oh, bliss! She felt her hand in his, warm and strong, and felt faint with it. She couldn't speak, could only go along with him, her feet wading through the hot sand beside him.

He went up to the attendant and chatted to him. They discussed various boards, and then he selected two. A beginner's board for her, and something very racy-looking for him.

'The wind's too light in the morning for anyone but beginners, but I haven't been out for a while,' he told her. 'So let's see how you're doing.' He held her board out to her, then turned to lift down the sails from their racks.

'Um, I'm not very good yet,' she managed to get out, as he fixed the sails onto the boards and checked they were stable.

He flashed a grin at her. 'After one lesson? How could you be? OK, let's go.'

The next hour passed in a blur of dazed, incandescent bliss. She was still totally useless at windsurfing, but she didn't care. Didn't care in the slightest. Because this time— this time Nikos Kiriakis was teaching her.

And the bliss of that was indescribable.

There were just so many opportunities for him to be fantastically, excitingly, intoxicatingly close to her. Running through the sail-raising manoeuvre on the sand and in the shallows. Helping her get her balance. Helping her back on her board when she fell off—several times. Helping her raise her sail again.

Today she made better progress. Not much, but a bit. He said as much as they finally headed to shore.

'You just need more practice,' he told her.

'About a million years of it!' She laughed ruefully.

'Maybe not quite that long.' He paused. 'But close…'

She laughed, not caring, and then suddenly she became aware that he was looking not at her face but at the way her wet T-shirt was clinging to her breasts.

And suddenly, quite suddenly, the humour vanished from her face.

She felt her breasts tighten. Felt it as distinctly, as clearly, as if a bell had rung. Felt her nipples puckering, visibly standing out through the clinging material of her bikini top and the T-shirt.

And then his eyes were being dragged away from her breasts—and up to her eyes.

For a long, helpless moment she gazed at him, while her body bloomed for him.

'Nikos—' Her voice was a thread.

He gave a small, minute smile, and she felt her breath still.

Then, with a flicker of his eyes, he was hefting up the board and carrying it to the rack. He came back to repeat the action for hers, and when everything was restored he turned to her and said, 'Lunch.'

They ate at the beach bar that did lunchtime snacks. He drank a beer, she a glass of white wine. It went to her head like champagne.

And so did Nikos Kiriakis.

It was heaven to have him again. Heaven to watch his eyes, his face, the strong column of his throat, the broad strength of his shoulders. Heaven to gaze at him, listen to his deep, accented voice, hear his laugh, watch his smile. Heaven to feel his eyes caress her…

Heaven, heaven, heaven.

Her heart sang like an uncaged bird.

If I have nothing else, she thought, I have this!

And then, as he pushed his coffee cup away from him, his eyes lifted to hers. There was no caress in them. His voice as he spoke sounded brisk and businesslike.

As if he'd just moved a million miles away from her.

'I'm afraid I have to go now, Janine. I've sorted out my business here. The estate agents know what I want by way of a villa, and will keep me informed, and all my business appointments are complete. I have to get back to Athens. I'm flying out this afternoon.'

It was like a dagger. A dagger plunging right inside her.

She swallowed. It was like swallowing fire.

'Of…of course…'

His eyes flickered over her. 'It's been good knowing you, Janine.' The way his voice slid over the initial J, softening it to a 'zh', made her heart contract. He got to his feet. He seemed very tall. Very far away already. The dagger was sliding deeper inside. He looked down at her a moment. Then lightly, very lightly, he bent and let his lips just brush hers.

'Goodbye.' His voice was soft. He straightened. His mouth tugged in a little smile as he looked down at her. 'Don't forget your windsurfing.'

She shook her head wordlessly. He beckoned to the barman, signing the chit with rapid scrawl.

For one last time he looked at her. Was there anything in his eyes? Anything at all? She couldn't see. Could only know that hers were straining up at him, that her skin felt cold and clammy in the heat. That something was happening to her that she could not bear.

He raised a hand. The game was just getting interesting. 'Take care.'

Was there a husk in his voice? The slightest sign of regret?

He gave her one last brief smile and headed off.

She watched him go until she could see him no longer.

It was bad. It was worse than bad. She paced on her balcony. Above her, the cold stars blazed, giving no comfort. There was none to give.

She pressed her fingers to her mouth, as if she could keep all her feelings pressed down inside her.

She should be grateful. Grateful he'd gone. Removed temptation. The terrible, overpowering temptation to fall for him.

She tried desperately to rationalise it. She'd been here, in a foreign land, in an emotionally charged state after encountering Stephanos, and then a man like Nikos Kiriakis had walked in, looking like every woman's fantasy male. Sex on legs. The most devastating man she'd ever seen, oozing sex appeal from every pore, totally and effortlessly gorgeous! No wonder she had reacted to him! She'd spent her adult life avoiding any chance of such entanglements.

And she'd succeeded. Succeeded completely—till now. Nikos Kiriakis had simply knocked away her defences as if they had been made of paper!

She stared out over the dark mass of the gardens. Starlight gleamed dimly on the surface of the pool.

Wanting Nikos Kiriakis.

For the first time in her life she wanted a man, wanted *him*, Nikos Kiriakis. Only him, only him—and she didn't have him.

She was woken by the phone ringing. It was scarcely dawn. She groped for the receiver, feeling bleary and disoriented. For one terrible yearning moment she thought it was Nikos.

It was Stephanos.

He was brief—agitatedly brief. It was late night in New York. They would be going to stay with friends on Long Island in a few days—the wedding he'd told her about. He couldn't speak long—he was snatching a few stolen moments. Was she all right? That was all he wanted to know. All he had time to ask. He had to go. She was in his thoughts, his darling girl. She must take care... He had to go...

The line went dead.

She lay back, receiver slack on her chest. She'd hardly been able to say a word. Just get out the assurance he needed. She felt bruised, dazed.

Slowly, dully, she replaced the receiver. She had wanted it to be Nikos. So, so much. She wanted anything she could get of him—anything, on any terms. Even if it was nothing more than a single night in his arms...

She rolled over, hugging herself in misery.

You aren't even going to get that! Hasn't he made it clear enough? He voted with his feet. He said goodbye and left. You are simply unimportant to him.

The knowledge ached through her. Ached all the way through the next few sleepless hours until at last, with slow dreariness, she got up. An early-morning swim, a long shower, washing her hair, her underwear, hanging it dripping on her balcony, gazing out blindly over the sea. Then finally, drearily, getting dressed in the first things that came to hand, and going downstairs to breakfast, to pick at food that tasted like sawdust, drink coffee that tasted like dishwater—all with that same slow, dull dreariness, that same slow, dull ache all the way through her.

Nikos had gone. She wanted him, and he had gone.

She stared down blindly into her coffee cup.

A pair of dark glasses landed on the tablecloth beside her. Someone sat down opposite her.

Her head started up.

She froze, not believing her eyes. Just not believing.

Dark gold-flecked eyes rested on her. Burning through her.

'I couldn't stay away from you,' said Nikos Kiriakis.

The motor yacht at anchor in the harbour at Skarios Town gleamed like a sleek white monster. A Greek flag fluttered from its stern, flapping blue and white.

'Not a sail to set or a tiller to pull. And a crew to turn on the engine and steer!'

'It's my kind of boat!' said Janine with a laugh.

Not a word had been spoken about Nikos's return. Not one. He had simply said, 'After breakfast I've got a surprise for you.'

He wouldn't tell her what, had just let a smile play around his mouth.

She'd gone with him in a dream. Floating off the ground. Her heart had been singing. Soaring. In her room she'd ripped off the T-shirt and shorts she'd put on so listlessly an hour ago and riffled through everything in her wardrobe. In the end she'd grabbed a sleeveless white sundress, completely impractical for the beach, but now, as he ushered her aboard this millionaire's monster, she knew it was ideal. The breeze winnowed her hair, floating it around her head like a maenad's.

She stared, wide-eyed, at the luxury on board as he led the way up to the sundeck above the cabin. Two loungers were set out beneath a stretched white awning, and Nikos settled her in one as if he had been handing her to a throne.

Janine sat down and gazed around her. A mix of fishing boats and sailing yachts bobbed about in the harbour, but there was nothing to compare with this floating monster. She felt the deck start to vibrate and saw the swirl of water that indicated the propeller was turning. One of the crew loosened the moorings and then jumped lightly aboard, gangplank already retracted. The boat started to nose away from the quayside.

As they gained the open sea and the yacht started to speed up she turned to Nikos.

'This is fantastic!'

He flashed a smile at her. He'd known she would be impressed. Who wouldn't be? He had chartered the cruiser in Patra and had her sailed over for this morning. Ready for his return from Athens.

It had been a nuisance having to detour to Athens yesterday, even though it had allowed him to drop in at his office and catch up with various business matters in person. But leaving Skarios—and Janine Fareham—had been a necessary part of his carefully calculated blow hot/blow cold strategy. And it had worked perfectly, he could see. As he'd walked up to her at breakfast she'd been sitting there like a forlorn, wilted flower, dejection and rejection in every line of her slender body.

The transformation as he announced his presence had been total.

She'd revived instantly, immediately. Incandescently. A glow of wonder had lit her face, her eyes, parted her lips. Shining from her like the sun.

Dazzling him.

He'd felt a kick go through him like a blow to his solar plexus.

Theos mou, but she was so beautiful! Her eyes alight, glowing with pleasure, her smile so radiant it all but knocked him over.

Satisfaction filled him. She was ready for him now.

And he, oh, he was more than ready for her.

It had been hard, much harder than he'd envisaged, to walk out on her yesterday. He'd had to force himself to his feet, force himself to smile down at her and tell her that he had to go back to Athens. And as for kissing her...

That had been hardest of all—to confine himself to nothing more than the most fleeting brush of his lips when he'd wanted to haul her up against him and ravish her warm, honeyed mouth with his...

Instead he'd had to straighten and saunter off, as if he hadn't got a single thought in his head except getting to the airport.

But now, ah, now it was a different story. He would not be leaving Janine Fareham again—not until he had tasted every ounce of honey she had to give.

And she would have so much! His eyes washed over her as she lay back in the lounger, lifting her face to the sunlight filtering through the awning, her long, beautiful hair flowing in the wind. His gaze stroked her, taking in the little details of her beauty—the delicate arch of her narrow feet in their strappy sandals, the elegant ankles, slender calves, honeyed thighs, and her wand-like waist, and those two sweet, gently swelling breasts, and her sculpted shoulders, her graceful neck, delicate jawline, tender earlobes and the long sweep of her eyelashes...

Why the hell did she have to be mixed up with Stephanos?

The thought came out of nowhere, hitting him like a blow as he realised how he had phrased that question. It should be the other way round. It should be *Why the hell did Stephanos have to be mixed up with her?*

But it hadn't come to him like that. Suddenly it had been Stephanos he resented, not Janine Fareham.

Janine.

He felt a smile hover at his mouth. Janine. Zhanine.

He liked saying her name, liked the way her name

sounded. And he liked the way *she* liked him saying it, with that soft 'zh' pronunciation that Greek gave it. The English pronunciation was harsh and ugly in comparison. Zhanine…

Much better. Much, much better…

His eyes flickered over her blonde loveliness again. Though her skin was tanned, she was completely un-Greek in appearance. He let his gaze rest on her. There was something familiar about her, he felt, with a strange flickering of memory. Who was it? It was not obvious, but every now and then there was something about her that made him think she looked like someone he knew.

He shook his head minutely. No, it was simply that he hadn't seen her in thirty-six hours and her beauty was stunning his senses again. That was all. It was just because he wanted to have her. Not because she resembled anyone he knew.

A sound of footsteps behind him made him turn. One of the crew was coming up to the sundeck, carrying a silver tray bearing two long-stemmed flutes and a bottle of freshly opened champagne nestling in an ice bucket. He set it down on a table between the loungers. Nikos nodded his thanks and the man took his leave.

Janine half sat up.

'Oh, I adore champagne!' she cried, her face lighting.

'I thought you might,' murmured Nikos, and poured her out a glass, and one for him, handing her the former. She took it with a grateful smile.

The chill, gently fizzing golden liquid iced beautifully down her throat, and Janine sighed with pleasure as she tasted the distinctive biscuity dryness of vintage champagne. It went perfectly with the bliss she was feeling. Had been feeling ever since Nikos had returned. She heard again, singing in her head, those blissful words—*I couldn't stay away from you…*

They had made her decision for her. She knew it, and she accepted it.

I couldn't stay away from you...

The words circled in her mind, making her heart swell.

I couldn't stay away from you...

Well, she couldn't stay away from him either. Whatever was happening, whatever was lifting her heart like this, whatever was making her breathless—heart racing, giddy with intoxication—whatever it was, she would go with it.

She would not be sensible.

It was far, far too late for that.

I can't think about anything else. Or anyone else.

Just Nikos.

Just Nikos.

She wouldn't question, wouldn't ask, wouldn't doubt or fear.

She would simply accept—and be glad, so glad.

She would go with him wherever he took her. Because she was helpless to do anything else.

She wanted only one thing—to be with Nikos Kiriakis.

Whatever happened.

CHAPTER FIVE

THE cruiser made its way northwards, leaving the shoreline of the island to port. Janine lay back and enjoyed the sensation, just as she enjoyed the exquisite flavour of the vintage champagne in her glass—and the even more exquisite pleasure of having Nikos Kiriakis beside her.

Sailing away with her.

He was watching her, she knew. She could feel it. It was almost tangible, the way his gaze set her nerve-ends quivering, vibrating finely in a way that was far more than the resonant vibration of the cruiser's engine. She wanted to turn her head and meet his eyes, knew that if she did the quivering would leap, sending her heart-rate skittering away. She felt breathless, intoxicated. And it was not the champagne—it was him, *him*, Nikos Kiriakis, pulling her towards him, drawing her inexorably towards him, and she could not hold back, could not resist him.

As the cruiser headed onwards, its sleek lines propelled by its powerful, throbbing engine, she felt that that was what Nikos was doing to her. Propelling her onwards, taking her with him. And she could not say no. Could not resist.

Where was he taking her? Where would their journey end?

She did not know, did not want to ask, was content to be swept along wherever he wanted her to go.

She had put herself in his hands.

She glanced back to the island across the churning of the wake. It seemed very far away.

Just like the rest of her life.

The only reality was here, now, with Nikos.

She tried to think of Stephanos, but he was so far away too. He slipped away from her mind, fading, dwindling.

She had longed so much for Nikos, dreamt of him, yearned for him and ached for him.

And he had come back to her.

She took another sip of champagne and let intoxication take her. The wind streamed over her face; the sun dazzled her eyes. She felt the cruiser alter direction subtly, felt the helm going a few points to port. Then they were rounding the island, starting to curve back south again, with the sun shifting direction.

'Are we going to go back around to the hotel?' Janine asked.

She looked across at Nikos and felt the now-familiar lurch of her heart at setting eyes on him. He was wearing his dark glasses, and glamour just oozed from him. What was it about dark glasses that made a man look so damn sexy? she found herself thinking. And on a man as sexy as Nikos in the first place the effect was devastating!

She hardly heard his answer, so rapt she was by gazing at his gorgeousness.

'Not quite that far,' he answered.

'So where, then?' she pressed.

But he would not answer, only let an enigmatic smile play around his mouth in a way that made her more riveted than ever, and quite took her mind off the mystery of where they were going to have lunch. So far as she knew there were no villages along that north-west shore—nothing until you reached Stephanos's hotel complex, which was just north of a tiny fishing village.

But it wasn't a village they were heading for—or even a hotel.

After following the dramatically rocky shoreline of the north-west coast, the cruiser suddenly veered inshore. For a while Janine could not see where on earth they might be heading. Apart from a rocky death upon the sea-washed cliffs. But then as they got closer and cleared another head-land she saw, nestling in its shelter, a tiny cove, gleaming with sand in a tiny half-moon, bordered by a simple stony quay running out from a track that wound up the cliffside. And as her eyes lifted she saw a sight that made her gasp.

A villa was perched on the crest of the cliff, so cunningly landscaped into the contours that it hardly showed from the sea. Only the sunshine dazzling on its windows gave away its existence.

Janine turned to Nikos.

'We're heading *there*?'

Nikos nodded. 'The agent sent me details—it sounded intriguing.'

It also, he thought, but did not say, sounded ideal for his purpose. Its remoteness was perfect.

There was a strange look in her eyes suddenly.

'Is—is that why you came back?' she asked. 'Just to view this villa?'

He heard the catch of doubt in her voice.

His eyelids drooped.

'No,' he said softly.

For a long moment he held her eyes, and he saw the colour stain out across those high, beautiful cheekbones un-til she looked away in confusion.

More than confusion.

Relief.

They drew nearer the shore, into the lee of the cliff, until they were able to moor along the quayside. As Janine walked down the short gangplank she felt the swell of the sea against the stone quay unbalance her slightly. She had nearly two glasses of champagne inside her, and had not yet eaten, and she swayed, catching at the guidebars on either side.

Hands steadied her at her waist, warm through the thin cotton of her sundress. Her heart gave a flutter and she paused, regaining her balance, then glanced back over her shoulder.

'Thanks.'

Her breath caught. Nikos—towering over her, his height accentuated by the slope of the gangplank—seemed over-whelming. His eyes were still shielded by his dark glasses, making her focus on that beautiful sculpted mouth of his, the lean outline of his jaw. For a second time stilled, and she felt as if she were drowning, unable to draw breath. She could feel the imprint of his hands on her, holding her still. He seemed so close to her—so close…

Oh, dear God, what is happening to me?

Emotion surged in her, sweeping through her like a wave. She felt herself sway again, and this time it had nothing to do with the sea, with the champagne. This was emotion trembling through her.

But what emotion?

Desperately she tried to give it a name. Intoxication? Wonder? Wanting?

Whatever it was it surged through her, unstoppable, mak-ing her weak, so weak…

A crewman was standing on the quay, dutifully holding out a hand to her to help her off. She stepped forward. Nikos's hands released her. The moment passed and she forced herself to recover some semblance of composure.

But as she fell into step beside Nikos she could feel her heart racing.

She glanced ahead of her. Judging by the way the rough track led off the shore end of the quay, winding up the lowest portion of the cliff to the right of the villa, it was going to be a steep climb. There seemed to be a stone hut of some description at the base of the track, with double doors like a garage. Maybe there was a Jeep inside or some-thing? Janine wondered.

She didn't get to find out.

'Come,' said Nikos, and led the way forward. Not to the

unmetalled track, but across the head of the tiny cove beyond the quay.

Janine gazed about her. It was exquisitely lovely, a perfect, tiny jewel of a beach, with golden sand and azure sea, backed by limestone cliffs tumbling with greenery, and tiny wavelets breaking in miniature foam. At the far end of the beach, where the cliff was sheer, she realised there was a kind of glass pod set against vertical rails, soaring upwards. It was, she realised, amazed, a lift.

Her lips parted in wonder as, after she was ushered inside by Nikos, they soared upwards. As they gained the villa level her lips stayed parted in wonder. A fantastic expanse of glittering blue water greeted her—an infinity pool set so cunningly into the terraced rock that as she looked it seemed to merge with the sea and the sky.

'Come,' said Nikos again. He led the way around the head of the pool, lightly ascending a shallow flight of steps that led to the villa itself.

It was very low and modern. Built in gleaming white stone, its wide expanse of sea-fronting windows dazzled in the sunlight.

Janine gazed about her, open-mouthed.

'Let me show you around,' said Nikos.

He slid open one of the vast pairs of windows and she walked inside. Again, the décor was startlingly modern— white and low and totally minimalist—and totally stunning. Polished wooden floors offset the white walls and furniture, and a pair of huge stone *pithoi* stood like sentinels at the far end.

Her sandals clacking noisily on the wooden floor, she followed him, still open-mouthed, as he showed her round the rest of the villa. It was all on one level, and from every room the same incredible view out over the sea greeted her. The huge bedroom had its own terrace and she wandered out, gazing at the spectacular view all around.

'This is an incredible place!'

The Harlequin Reader Service® — Here's how it works:

Accepting your 2 free books and gift places you under no obligation to buy anything. You may keep the books and gift and return the shipping statement marked "cancel." If you do not cancel, about a month later we'll send you 6 additional books and bill you just $3.80 each in the U.S., or $4.47 each in Canada, plus 25¢ shipping & handling per book and applicable taxes if any.* That's the complete price and — compared to cover prices of $4.50 each in the U.S. and $5.25 each in Canada — it's quite a bargain! You may cancel at any time, but if you choose to continue, every month we'll send you 6 more books, which you may either purchase at the discount price or return to us and cancel your subscription.

*Terms and prices subject to change without notice. Sales tax applicable in N.Y. Canadian residents will be charged applicable provincial taxes and GST.

If offer card is missing write to: The Harlequin Reader Service, 3010 Walden Ave., P.O. Box 1867, Buffalo, NY 14240-1867

NO POSTAGE
NECESSARY
IF MAILED
IN THE
UNITED STATES

BUSINESS REPLY MAIL

FIRST-CLASS MAIL   PERMIT NO. 717-003   BUFFALO, NY

POSTAGE WILL BE PAID BY ADDRESSEE

HARLEQUIN READER SERVICE
3010 WALDEN AVE
PO BOX 1867
BUFFALO NY 14240-9952

Do You Have the LUCKY KEY?

PLAY THE Lucky Key Game

and you can get

FREE BOOKS *and a* FREE GIFT!

Scratch the gold areas with a coin. Then check below to see the books and gift you can get!

DETACH AND MAIL CARD TODAY!

YES! I have scratched off the gold areas. Please send me the **2 FREE BOOKS** and **GIFT** for which I qualify. I understand I am under no obligation to purchase any books, as explained on the back of this card.

(H-P-10/05)

306 HDL D7ZE   106 HDL D72F

FIRST NAME

LAST NAME

ADDRESS

APT.#

CITY

STATE/PROV.

ZIP/POSTAL CODE

2 free books plus a free gift   1 free book

2 free books   Try Again!

Offer limited to one per household and not valid to current Harlequin Presents® subscribers. All orders subject to approval. Credit or Debit balances in a customer's account(s) may be offset by any other outstanding balance owed by or to the customer.

www.eHarlequin.com

© 2002 HARLEQUIN ENTERPRISES LTD. ® and ™ are trademarks owned and used by the trademark owner and/or its licens

'It is, is it not? And now that we are here let us enjoy what it has to offer. Beginning—' he smiled down at her '—with lunch.'

Her eyes widened. 'Is that allowed?'

'The villa is at my disposal,' he answered, as if the very idea that Nikos Kiriakis should not be allowed to do something he wanted to do was absurd. 'Now, would you care to freshen up?' He indicated the *en suite* bathroom off the main bedroom.

'Well, if you say it's OK,' she said doubtfully.

'Of course.' He smiled again.

She went off to make the most of the palatial facilities. When she emerged she headed down the little flight of steps that led from the bedroom terrace down to the main terrace, beside the infinity pool. As she descended she saw that the crew had set out a table with a huge canvas sunshade overhead, and were now busy unloading what looked to be half a dozen picnic hampers. Nikos was lounging against a stone balustrade, gazing out over the incredible view of the sea.

For a moment she just stood, gazing at him. Her heart seemed to still.

He turned and smiled at her, and held out his hand.

She went to join him.

The food was exquisite—delicate trifles that melted in the mouth, morsel after morsel, tempting and irresistible. Dessert was even more delicious, and Janine did not even try and say no to the iced almond parfait in its crystal bowl. Spoonful by tiny spoonful she consumed it, sighing with pleasure.

Nikos sat back and watched her through half-closed enigmatic eyes.

She felt his gaze on her, heavy and sensual.

'I can't eat another mouthful—'

Reluctantly Janine set down her dessert spoon, pushing the half-finished dessert away from her and leaning back in her director's chair, tilting back the rest, stretching out her legs. She reached for her glass of sweet Sauternes wine. On top of the glass of Chablis Nikos had persuaded her to drink, and the champagne earlier, she could feel the wine soothing through her body.

Her limbs felt heavy, languorous. Heat licked at her skin. A tiny breeze toyed with the tendrils of her hair, playing over her bare shoulders, her bare arms. The Sauternes slipped down her throat like honey, and she sighed again with pleasure.

She felt replete. The combination of wine and heat made her feel dreamy, indolent. She didn't want to move. Not for a long time. Perhaps not for ever. She wanted time to hold still, the way it was doing now. So she could go on being here, now, with this man, beneath the azure sky, heat beating over her like a slow pulse.

She gave another long, pleasurable sigh, and relaxed back even more in her chair.

'I could stay here for ever,' she murmured. 'It's so peaceful. So beautiful.' She turned her head to smile sleepily at Nikos. 'Thank you for bringing me here,' she said softly. Then, even more softly, 'Thank you for coming back…'

He gave a half-smile back, that same enigmatic look in his eyes. She let him look at her, let his gaze entwine with hers. There was silence all around them. Silence and the sweet scent of white jasmine drifting through the air. She was holding his eyes still, and they seemed very dark. She could see the flecks of gold deep within.

He reached and stroked her arm. It felt like the drift of swansdown on her skin.

She ought to move her arm. Ought to tell him not to do what he was doing. But the drift of his fingers was too lovely.

She saw his eyelids droop, saw the enigmatic half-smile pull at his mouth—that beautiful, sensual, sculpted mouth.

'Nikos…' She breathed his name.

His fingers went on drifting over her skin.

Her eyes twined with his.

'I came back,' he said softly, 'because I could not stay away.'

She said nothing, could say nothing, though her eyes were wide and wondering.

His fingers went on drifting, stroking. They slid over her wrist, holding her. His thumb circled slowly over the delicate skin over her veins. His eyes held hers, slow-burning coals, flecked with golden flame.

He got to his feet, drawing her up with him. She came with him, helpless to resist. The wine sang in her blood, low and sweet. The warmth caressed her skin. The sun beat down on her, making her weak.

His hands slipped over her shoulders, warm and heavy.

He lowered his head to her mouth.

His kiss was everything she had dreamt it would be. Slow, and sensuous, tasting her like wine.

And she gave herself to it.

The world slowed. Time stopped. His mouth moved on hers and she was drowning, drowning. Bliss ran in her veins like slow, sweet honey.

Weakness washed over her, wave after wave. Her muscles had no strength. Her will had no strength. She was caught in his arms, her hands touching the contours of his shoulders, her breasts pillowed on his chest. She could feel her nipples prickling, feel the little shivers of arousal teasing through her veins. His hands moved across her back, stroking her, as his mouth moved softly, so softly, over hers. The wave of weakness washed through her again.

I can't resist him, she thought. I can't, I can't.

It's too late for resistance, too late for regrets. I thought he had gone, that he did not want me. But he came back to me and I cannot, cannot, say no to him. Not now, not now. Madness it may be, but it's too late, too late.

'Nikos…'

She breathed his name into his mouth and the world slid away. Her hands slipped upwards, winding around his neck, holding his head to hers as her mouth opened to his and his tongue eased within.

The flush of desire coursed through her body; the sun beat on her back. Her swollen breasts felt heavy, ripening against him. His hands slipped down to her hips and then, as if she were no more than a feather, he gathered her up.

He took her indoors. Her head hung bowed, heavy, upon his shoulder as he carried her, her body limp and weak in his arms. Inside was cooler, the shaded bedroom cooler still, and he laid her down upon the wide bed.

She lay, her sundress riding up her thighs, one strap half-descended from her shoulder. Her heart was slewing in thick, heavy beats.

For one long, endless moment she lay there as he stood quite still and looked down at her. In the shadows of the room she could not read his eyes. His face was taut. Only the pulse at his throat betrayed his condition.

He reached a hand down to her. But it was not to touch her body. Only the thin, strappy sandals. He slid them off her bare feet and tossed them away. Then he stood back again.

'Perfect,' he said softly. 'Quite, quite perfect.'

His gaze laced over her, just as it had done the first time he had ever set eyes on her, she knew. But now—now he would do more than look. He had set her body alight that very first time he had stood looking down at her, so near naked in her bikini. And that same hot flame shimmered within her now.

'Nikos,' she breathed again, helpless in desire.

She wanted him so much. Wanted that lean, hard, male strength pressing on her, possessing her.

A smile curved at his mouth and she felt her breath catch. He plunged his hand into his trouser pocket with slow deliberation and took out a handful of silvery packets. With the same carelessness with which he had treated her unnecessary sandals, he tossed them down on the bedside table.

He smiled down at her again. Her eyes had widened. He started to unbutton his shirt. She lay there, watching him undress, watching his beautiful, lean body emerge, her eyes feasting on him with helpless desire. As he removed the last of his clothing she saw just how very, very aroused he was.

He paused, reaching for one of the packets, and sheathed himself. Then, with that same slow deliberation, he came towards her.

A smile was playing around his mouth.

So this, thought Janine, in as much as she was capable of thinking, as her body melted around her, was what it was like to be seduced by Nikos Kiriakis.

Because that was what he was doing. Seducing her.

Touch by touch by touch.

How could she have thought he didn't want her? How could she possibly have thought that?

He stroked her limbs, hands gliding like silk along her bare arms, mouth lowering to graze along the fine ridge of her collarbone, before moving softly, exquisitely, across her throat, to nuzzle at her tender earlobes. She sighed with pleasure, feeling herself melting beneath his silken caresses. He teased her lips with his, easing them open, stroking her tongue with his as she opened beneath him.

And as he did so he slid the half-fallen strap from her shoulder and softly peeled the fine material of her dress away from her swelling breast.

His fingers played with her a little, skimming the delicate underswell, grazing the aching tip, until she moaned, neck arching. His lips left hers and his head bowed, mouth closing over her straining nipple instead. He suckled her softly, oh, so softly, and the little moans in her throat came again and again.

'Do you like that?' he murmured, smiling as his mouth left her breast and then, his gold-flecked eyes holding hers, which gazed up at him, wide and dilated, he moved his hand to her other shoulder, lifting away her other strap and taking it down her arm to expose her other breast.

He paused a moment, his eyes breaking with hers to gaze down upon her nakedness, edged with the white material of her half-removed sundress.

'Such beautiful breasts,' he breathed, and his head lowered again.

Her fingers twisted in the bedclothes, and her spine strained upwards as he suckled her again.

Desire was dissolving her, dissolving her into a soft, boneless mass of sensation—such sweet, sweet sensation.

He went on suckling her, his tongue making soft circles around her nipple, each circle more blissful than the next. And as he laved her breasts his hand glided like silk along her leg, sliding under the rucked hem of her sundress, fingers hooking around the low-slung waistband of her panties.

He eased them down, lifting her hips enough to free them from the rounded globes of her bottom, and slid her legs free of them. And then his hand returned to her.

If she had thought she could know no further bliss, she discovered with a breathless parting of her lips just how much bliss was yet to come. With the delicate, skilful tips of his fingers he played with her a while, exploring each delicate fold, loosening her, dewing her, readying her for his possession. And all the while his mouth worked its magic upon her breasts.

She was quivering with desire—aching with it, melting with it.

'Nikos—'

His name was an exhalation. An invocation. A plea.

He lifted his head and looked into her eyes. In the dim light they were deep, dilated pools. He smoothed his hand over her forehead. She gazed up at him, helpless with her desire. For one long, long moment he looked down at her.

She could not see his eyes. His face was shadowed, only the contours of his features visible.

He was the most beautiful man in the world.

'Nikos…' She breathed his name again, whispering it. Her thighs slackened as his hand moved from her, easing her legs apart.

He lifted himself and slowly, teasingly slow, glided into her, so smooth, so powerful that he filled her absolutely, completely.

For a moment, a brief, timeless moment, he stilled, and she could feel her muscles strain around him, enclosing him. Her fingers hovered on the smooth, warm skin of his shoulders.

Then with absolute control he moved within her.

She felt the exquisite pleasure of his movement within her, stroking her, caressing her with the most intimate part of himself.

She sighed, sweet and susurrating.

Her eyes fluttered shut and she gave herself to the sensation. Her hands folded over his shoulders, feeling their strength, the smoothness of his skin, the muscles layered beneath.

So beautiful. He was so sublime, so male. And what he was doing to her was beyond words.

She breathed again, exhaling slowly, then breathing in again, taking him with her as she did so.

He went on stroking her, caressing her, and her body became one single point of sensation, just there, *there*, where her sensitivity was greatest, her arousal most exquisite.

She breathed his name again, her head moving slowly, as if submerged, and then, as if a slow underwater wave were welling through her, her body undulated. The sweetest honey was oozing through every vein, every nerve, reaching up, and up, and up—and releasing, out, out into her skin, her flesh, suffusing her body with one long, endless welling of sensation so exquisite she exhaled in a long, endless sighing.

And then, just as she felt the sensation begin to ebb, making her ache with the loss of it, he moved once more within her, and then again, in one slow, final, releasing surge, and the sensation was released in him, so it came again in her, again and again, over and over, wave after wave, sweetness after sweetness, until her body was a fusion of it, and nothing existed, could exist, would ever exist again. Her whole body was one exquisite, endless wave of sensation.

To the end, the very end, she let the sweet, honeyed wave carry her, oblivious to everything else, existing only in her own exquisite bliss. Until at last, at last it was no more, no last drop of honey remained.

She gave a long, languorous sigh, limbs slackening, muscles releasing.

Her eyelids fluttered. She should open her eyes, she thought dimly, vaguely. But her eyelids were too heavy, her limbs were too heavy.

'Nikos?' Her voice was a sigh.

A hand smoothed over her forehead.

'Shh…' he murmured.

'It was so beautiful…'

She felt his mouth on hers, soft and tender. Then he was coming down beside her, folding her to him, enclosing her.

'Nikos…' she breathed again.

His hand smoothed her thigh.

'So beautiful…'

Her eyes were heavy, limbs weak. Her breathing slowed, her heart rate calmed, and the warm peace of sleep crept over her.

*   *   *

Nikos watched her sleep, a smile curving his mouth. Her breasts rose and fell gently. They were soft again, soft and very beautiful, their skin paler than the surrounding flesh. His smile deepened. She could sunbathe nude here. There would be no one to see. The villa was his. He had bought it the day before yesterday, fully furnished, at the asking price. The agent had not been able to believe his luck. Nikos hadn't cared. One of the business appointments that he had used as an excuse to stay away from Janine that second day had been to take a helicopter trip here, to check it out. He had bought it on the spot.

It was too beautiful not to possess.

His hand reached to smooth Janine's golden hair. Just as she was too beautiful not to possess.

A deep satisfaction filled him. He tried to remember the anger he'd felt about her, but it seemed impossible to recall. And it was irrelevant now, anyway. Janine would never go back to Demetria's husband—he had seen to that, irrevocably. His satisfaction deepened.

He curled a thread of hair around his finger. She really was so very, very lovely. Her body had melted around his, taking him with her in a fusion of the senses.

It had been good. Quite extraordinarily good.

He gave a soft, silent laugh. He had intended the experience to be incredible for her, not for him. That was, after all, the whole purpose of the exercise. To seduce her.

But she had made it incredible for him too.

He still wasn't really sure how. She had done nothing except accept everything he did to her. Absorb every sensation he aroused in her. Absorb it deep, deep within her. Then radiate it out again, as if she were molten in his arms.

It had been the intensity of her responsiveness that had aroused him so much, he realised. No other woman had ever responded to him like that.

He wanted to feel that response again.

He shifted position. He could feel his body reacting to that thought. He eased further back. Whatever he might want to do, first he must visit the bathroom. Then, when he returned, it would be time—oh, yes, time to rouse Janine from her slumber.

'Do you mean it? Do you really mean it?'

Janine's eyes were like stars.

Nikos raised his hand in a very Greek gesture. 'Of course. Why else should I have said we would stay here?'

'But your work—don't you have to be back in Athens?'

He shrugged. 'The villa is fully equipped—I can be on-line to my office whenever I choose. It will do perfectly well for a while. And I didn't buy this villa so that I would never get to spend time here!'

She shook her head. 'I still can't believe you bought a place like this just like that!'

He looked surprised. 'Why not? The villa is spectacular—and as an asset it will only increase in value. Property prices on Skarios are rising steadily as the island opens up for more tourism. It is a good investment. And—' his eyes washed purposefully over Janine '—it affords the privacy we need.'

He lowered his head to kiss her again. They were leaning, side by side, on the balustrade overlooking the pool. The sun had set. Above their heads the stars were pricking out, one by one. Ahead, the darkening sky was faintly tinged with a golden streak along the horizon.

A light wind was winnowing their faces.

As Nikos's mouth moved softly on hers Janine dared not think, only feel. This was bliss. When Nikos had told her just now about the villa, told her that it was his, that they were to stay here together, she had scarce dared believe it.

'I told you,' he had said, kissing her softly, 'that I could not stay away from you.'

She had searched his eyes. His expression had been full.

'I want you very much,' he had said, as softly as his kiss.

And he did want her—she'd had proof of that all the long, hot afternoon. Even now, as they stood here, his arm around her, she could feel the afterglow of his desire for her—of hers for him—in every part of her body.

Wonder filled her. Wonder that what she had wanted so much had come to her! That Nikos had swept her away to this beautiful private place to make love to her.

The outer world ceased to exist. Had ceased to exist since the moment when he had first kissed her here, and she had known there was but one destination for her. His bed.

She had gone gladly, rapturously, putting everything aside except this—this consummation of her desire for him. He had cast a glamour over her, woven a spell to enchant her, captivate her. And she could not resist him.

She leant against him, feeling his strength, his warmth. His arm tightened around her shoulder. Around her the world stilled, the moment captured. Time had stopped. She never wanted it to start again.

Nikos leant back in the wooden-slatted padded steamer chair set out on the terrace above the pool, sipping his beer and watching Janine swim slowly up and down. Her naked body parted the water, gliding forward, her blonde hair streaming behind her like a mermaid's tresses, iridescent in the submerged lighting of the pool, which turned every brush of water to champagne and limned her body with gold.

A near full moon was riding in the sky. Crickets clicked in the vegetation. Down below, on the beach, he could hear the low murmur of the sea. The faint wash from Janine's breast-stroke was the only other sound.

They had the world to themselves.

It felt good. Very good.

He took another mouthful of beer. When he'd first come here the moon had been nothing but a silver sliver. Since then the days had passed, timeless, measured only by the sun and the moon, by the intervals between making love to Janine.

Janine…

He let her name play on his lips.

In the water her body moved with sensuous grace. He watched her, feeling desire germinate yet again deep in his being. When she emerged he would take her again. So many times now…and each coming together had been unforgettable. Sensual, incredibly sensual, and her extraordinary responsiveness to him, which had so amazed him that very first time, had never abated, never ebbed. Every, *every* time he took her it was there, intensifying the experience beyond words, beyond rational thought.

But it was more than her responsiveness. He searched for a word that would fit, but it was elusive. Then it came to him.

There was a *sweetness* about possessing Janine that he had never expected. How could he have? She was a woman who had attached herself to a wealthy, married and older man, who was threatening his sister's marriage. There was nothing of *sweetness* in such an activity!

A faint frown crossed his forehead. The woman he held in his arms each night seemed so very different from how such a woman should be. A woman who took rich married men for her lovers! Such a woman as that he might feel desire for, yes, but other than that, nothing but contempt and anger… Yet those two last emotions were not there any longer, he realised, wonderingly. His frown deepened. How could that be? Where had those dark emotions about Janine Fareham gone? Where was his anger at what she had done to Demetria? Where was his contempt for her affair with Stephanos?

Why was the only feeling he now had towards her simply…desire? Pure, burning, incandescent desire. More overwhelming than he had ever known for any woman. All consuming, all powerful.

Why? Why was the woman in his arms, his bed, so different from what he had expected her to be as Stephanos's mistress? Here, with him, she simply didn't seem to connect with such a female.

His brow furrowed again. What was going on? And worse, why did he trouble himself with it? Trying to discover why it was that he felt now only desire for Janine Fareham—a woman he should hate, should despise, for the way she lived her life. A thread of unease ran through him, disturbing him.

He didn't want to think about her affair with Stephanos. He wanted to blot it out. Once again, as on the cruiser, he found himself wanting to think of Janine as if she were not another man's mistress.

As if she were simply *his*.

A slow smile curved his mouth. Well, she was his now, all right. He had brought her here and made her his own.

His eyes rested on her as she glided silently, steadily, through the silken waters, beneath the silver light of the moon.

So very beautiful…a timeless image to remember.

That was all he had to focus on. The simple fact that he wanted Janine Fareham—desired her more than any woman he could remember—and that he had got her.

He took another sip of beer. As he moved his hand moonlight glinted on his watch. Time, he thought, was marching inexorably on. Bringing Stephanos back to Greece, to the moment of inevitable confrontation.

He was not looking forward to it. It would be messy, and unpleasant—but it had to be done. For Demetria's sake.

And when it was over? What then? What would he do with Janine Fareham?

His smile turned mocking. Self-mocking. He already knew very well what he would do with her.

He was going to keep her. He wanted her far, far too much to let her go.

He was captivated by her. Captivated by her beauty, her

sensuality, her sweetness. He admitted it. He hadn't wanted to be, but he was.

And he didn't want to fight it any more. Why should he?

He had achieved exactly what he'd set out to do—seduced Stephanos's mistress away from him and taken her himself. Whatever her reasons for having become his brother-in-law's mistress, she was finished with Stephanos now. He'd seen to that.

A stab of fierce, hard satisfaction went through him. Primitive, atavistic—and too powerful to deny. It might have been for Demetria's sake that he had started out on this course—but now he had a reason all of his own.

He wanted Janine for himself—and he didn't want Stephanos to have her.

The knowledge mocked him, but he didn't care. She had captivated him and that was that.

And where was the problem? There was no problem—Janine Fareham had been a problem only when she'd been a threat to his sister's happiness. That threat was over now—and he, *he* was free to enjoy her.

Desire her.

Sate himself on her.

Make her honeyed sweetness his own.

A sense of well-being eased through him. For as long as he wanted he would have Janine to himself. She was his, only his, from now on.

Nothing—and no one—could take her from him.

Janine walked along the sand. This early it felt cool to the touch, still shaded by the cliff from the morning light. Nikos was at his laptop, ensconced in the high-tech office, touching base with his affairs. For herself, she had time to wander on this beautiful, perfect gem of a private beach, letting the water wash around her feet as she walked slowly along, wondering at the happiness she felt. The air was clear, with not a breath of wind. The cruiser was gone from the quay, out on its daily journey to Skarios Town, where the crew picked up the provisions needed for the villa. Apart from when the chef came up to cook dinner, she and Nikos hardly saw them.

It was almost as if they were the only people in the world.

Like Adam and Eve, in a world new-made for them, and them alone.

She felt her heart squeeze. Something was happening to her, here in this beautiful, magical place. Something that overwhelmed her. That she could not deny, could not prevent. She halted, staring out to sea. The morning sun was pouring down upon its surface, making it too bright to look at. Little wavelets flowed over her bare feet.

Emotion welled through her.

An emotion she would not name. Dared not.

She didn't want to give it a name. Didn't want to admit it. Because what was the point of admitting it? She had given herself to Nikos because she could not have done otherwise. Because he desired her as intensely, as irresistibly as she desired him.

But there could be no future in it. None. She knew that. Knew it with a deep, deep pain that made her refuse to name the emotion that welled through her. He wanted her for now, that was all. He was as caught up with her as she with him, but for him, she knew with bleak certainty there would come a moment when it would be over.

And what was the point? Oh, what was the point of dreaming of something that could never be? Not for a man like Nikos Kiriakis, for whom women were an endless stream.

For a second—a brief, tantalising, excruciating moment—she allowed herself to dream. Dream of a happiness so great that it would make her current state of bliss negligible in comparison!

Supposing—oh, just supposing Nikos felt the same emotion she felt. That same emotion that must not speak its name…

Supposing—oh, just supposing Nikos should turn to her

and take her hand, tell her he wanted her to be part of his life…

For just a few precious moments she let herself imagine such a thing.

Then, with a sigh, she went on walking.

She would have this time with Nikos, this precious time—the days of exploring each other's minds, the nights their bodies. And no one could take it away from her. Nothing could spoil it. It would be a precious, beautiful memory. Nothing could destroy it.

Cradling a glass of cold, fresh orange juice in one hand, Janine slid back the huge glass doors of the living room and stepped out onto the terrace. Nikos was already there, sitting at the shaded table, drinking coffee and reading the morning's paper. It had been delivered a short time ago, when the cruiser had returned from Skarios Town. She drifted up to him, feeling warm and languorous, her silky robe wafting around her. When she had come up from the beach Nikos had finished with his e-mails—and he'd been hungry.

But not for breakfast. He'd gathered her up in his arms, peeling off the strap-tied suntop and shorts she'd worn down to the beach to walk along the sand. He'd led her back to bed. Desire had lit his eyes.

An eternity later he'd shaved and showered while she slept in the aftermath of their passion, and now she was finally emerging herself, her body honeyed and replete.

She kissed his hair, and he lifted his eyes briefly from the paper to smile fleetingly at her, then took her seat opposite him. The day was heating, and she felt the strength of the sun even through the parasol.

It would be another hot day.

She smiled to herself. Every day was hot. Every day sunny, cloudless. Every day a day in paradise. Like glowing pearls she gathered them on her rope of memory.

They would not last for ever, she knew that, but while

they lasted she would distil every last ounce of happiness she could, full and overflowing.

She sipped her orange juice, bringing her gaze back from the breathtaking vista all around, of sea and sky and dazzling white cliffs, of splashing green vegetation, the brilliant azure of the pool almost at her feet.

All my life, she thought. All my life I'll remember this. Sitting here like this, in the morning heat, with Nikos beside me.

Her eyes swept back to the paper Nikos was reading. In Greek, it was indecipherable. She gazed at the picture of the politician on the front cover as Nikos perused the report of some football match on the back page. She could read nothing—nothing except the date, written in numerals.

As the numbers swam in front of her eyes and resolved themselves she felt her heart plummet. How could it be that date already? How could the days have passed so quickly?

Foolish question! Time had seemed to stop here, in this beautiful, magical place, but in the rest of the world the clocks had kept on ticking.

Remorselessly.

She bit her lip. She might have wanted time to stop, but it hadn't. She might have wanted the outside world to disappear, but it hadn't.

And now it had returned. Stephanos had been due back yesterday.

She felt her heart contract. With Nikos she forgot everything but him! Everything—even Stephanos.

But Stephanos was her priority—he had to be. He could spend so little time with her, and she had to place him first. However magical this time with Nikos had been, she owed it to Stephanos to be there for him when he returned.

As for herself and Nikos?

Well, she'd answered that question already, down on the beach.

Resignation filled her. There could be no future for them. Nikos would move on to another woman, and she... Well, she would be left with bittersweet memories. And an emotion she would not name, which would surely, if it were left unfed, wither and die all on its own?

It would have to. Her time with Nikos was over. Suddenly, without her realising it, the hourglass had run its course and the sand was all gone. Her time with him was all gone.

All gone.

A sense of loss flooded through her.

Would she ever see Nikos again? He knew about her and Stephanos, so perhaps there might be a chance of encountering him again…

Yes, with his next woman on his arm.

She pressed her lips together, accepting that reality. She had had her time with Nikos. Now it was over.

And it was time to go back to Stephanos and be grateful, oh, so grateful, that she had him in her life now!

Nikos was folding the paper away, paying her some attention again. As his eyes lit on her he paused, seeing the strained expression on her face.

He frowned, concerned.

'What is it?'

She reached automatically for the coffeepot, jerkily.

'I've just seen the date.' She lifted her eyes to Nikos. She swallowed. 'Stephanos was due back yesterday.'

She poured out her coffee. Reality was crashing back. 'I've got to go back to the hotel. To be there for him. He can spend so little time with me—'

She looked at him, her expression troubled, then the words burst from her.

'I know I shouldn't have had this affair with you, Nikos. But you made it impossible for me to resist! I took one look at you and everything else just went out the window.' She gave a faint, rueful smile, trying so hard to be brave, though she felt like howling, weeping, crying, keening.

'This…this time with you has been magical, Nikos—truly magical! I'll never forget it—and I'll never regret it!'

He was looking at her. His expression was closed. She could not read it.

'But clearly,' he said, 'it meant very little to you.'

She stared. 'How can you think that? How *can* you?'

'What else am I to think?'

His voice was cold. A chill went through her. What was happening?

'What else am I to think?' he demanded again. 'You sit there and calmly tell me you are returning to the hotel to wait for Stephanos.'

She was bewildered, dismayed. 'But...but of course I must. You *must* know how much he means to me!'

His eyes were like gold chips. Hard. Anger was lashing through him. It had come out of nowhere, like a summer storm at sea, brought on by her words. Her serenely uttered words that told him, oh, so calmly, that she was returning to her protector.

'I had thought that you *must* know how much you mean to *me*!' His voice mocked her intonation.

She stilled. 'Do I? Do I, Nikos? Do I know what I mean to you? We've spent this time here—and it's been magical for me—magical!—like nothing else in my life! But what was it for you?'

Her eyes were wide, pained. And suddenly Nikos understood. She had no idea what he intended for her. The storm vanished from his eyes.

He got to his feet and came round to her. He drew her up, taking her hands in his. He looked down into her face. Her beautiful, captivating face. He was quite resolved now. Her talk of returning to Stephanos had made it crystal-clear in his mind. He wanted Janine still, and he would keep her. Even had her protector been anyone else he would still have wanted her, would still have kept her. His desire for her was as overpowering now as it had been when he had first taken her.

He was going to keep her, and nothing was going to stop him. Nothing and no one.

'I don't want to part with you, Janine,' he said softly, his eyes lambent. 'I want us to be together. I want to take you back to Athens with me and make you mine. Recognised by all the world as mine.'

She gazed up at him. The breath had frozen in her throat.

Was she hearing right? Was she really, really hearing right?

Of all the words in all the world, those were the ones she had most longed to hear—the ones that she had never, never thought she would.

The emotion that she so feared to name leapt in her heart.

Her face lit like sunlight within.

'Do you really mean that?'

Her voice was a whisper. Dared she believe him. Dared she?

Her heart was full, so full…

'Do you doubt me?' he countered. 'You've swept me away, Janine. Captivated me!' He gazed down at her. Her eyes were shining again, like stars. He liked that. He liked that a lot. He liked Janine gazing up at him with stars in her eyes. He lifted her hands to his mouth and kissed each one softly, tenderly. 'I don't care who you are. It doesn't matter to me. You are mine now, and that is all that I care about. And I want you to be my—'

He paused, listening. He could hear something. A faint, distinctive thudding. It came from the land.

She drew back a little. What had made him stop—and at such a moment?

Then she heard it too.

'What is that?' She sounded alarmed.

The noise was getting louder. Closer.

Nikos glanced at her, then up to the sky. The noise was getting almost intolerable now. 'It's a helicopter,' he said. 'It's coming in to land. There's a helipad behind the villa.'

'But who on earth—?' Her words were inaudible. The racket of the rotors was deafening this close, as the machine descended.

Nikos didn't bother to answer her. He knew with every instinct just who was in that helicopter. But no purpose would be served by telling Janine. She would find out in a moment anyway.

He steeled himself. This had come too soon. He'd wanted more time. But he should have known it would happen. If it had been him coming back to find that Janine had gone from him, been taken, he, too, would have been in the first helicopter here.

The noise of the rotors increased. So did the tension stealing through him.

This was not going to be pleasant. But it had to be done. Janine was his—his completely. There was no doubt of it in his mind. Not a shadow. Her reaction just now, to his telling her that he was taking her back to Athens with him, showed him that.

Stephanos was finished—and Nikos had his revenge and had saved his sister's marriage.

His mouth tightened in a grim line. All he had to do now was convince his sister's husband of that.

Convince him that his young mistress had taken a new lover—that he, Nikos, had taken her. And was keeping her.

His eyes glanced over Janine. She looked perfect. Just the way he wanted her to look. Ideal for his purpose. Hair tousled, wearing only a loose silk robe, skimming her beautiful body, her lips beestung from passion. No guesses as to how she had spent the night. Or—he closed his arm around her shoulders, pulling her tightly, intimately against his body—who with.

The change in the pitch of the rotors told him the helicopter had landed. The infernal racket cut out any other noise. He felt tension tighten all the way through him. He had to get through this ordeal, however ugly it proved. He had to convince Stephanos that Janine was finished with him.

'Nikos—what's happening? I don't understand?'

There was bewilderment in her voice. Did she really have

no clue who was about to storm in here like a SWAT team? Well, he thought grimly, it was too late to mount a rescue for her. Much, much too late.

And the lady didn't even *want* rescuing! Was perfectly happy right where she was. Had chosen *him*, Nikos. Was *his*. There was no going back for her. Not now.

Footsteps pounded on the stairs leading down from the helipad past the villa. Then suddenly he was there. He was breathing heavily, Nikos could see.

His eyes fell on the pair of them immediately, and he stopped dead. At his side Nikos could feel Janine freeze totally.

'Stephanos—' he greeted the other man smoothly in his own language. 'I thought it might be you. You really shouldn't have left such a delectable creature on her own the way you did. You have arrived too late. Much, much too late. Janine is with me now.' He swapped to English suddenly. He wanted Janine to get this message too. 'She's staying with me, Stephanos. I'm taking her back to Athens.'

He brushed his lips across the top of Janine's hair, caressing her shoulder as he smiled at the other man. It was like sticking a knife into Stephanos's gut. His brother-in-law's face had gone completely white.

Then another face swam in his mind. Demetria—gaunt, desperate, despairing. His heart hardened. Stephanos should never have caused her so much pain and grief. His hand tightened around Janine's shoulder.

'She was very easy to seduce, Stephanos...' he taunted softly. 'And so very rewarding.'

For an endless moment the tableau held. Then, with a roar, Stephanos launched himself forward.

'You dare,' he yelled, his face contorted with rage, 'you *dare* to stand there and boast to me of seducing my daughter?'

CHAPTER SIX

His fist flew forward, ramming right at Nikos's face. Janine screamed. Instinctively Nikos blocked, letting go of Janine as he did so and seizing Stephanos's forearm before his fist could impact.

'Daughter?' Nikos's voice was a hiss. 'Do you take me for a fool? Do you take your *wife* for a fool? My *sister*! My poor, wretched sister! Who begged me from her hospital bed to help her. Who wept in my arms because her husband was infatuated with a twenty-five-year-old girl he'd picked up at an airport! You took one look at her and she was in your bed the same day!'

There was a low moan from beside him. He ignored it. His face was contorted, as he still exerted all his force to hold Stephanos's striking arm away from him.

Abruptly Stephanos's fist dropped. He took a step back. The expression on his face was ghastly.

'You don't understand.' His voice was a hoarse rasp. 'Janine is my daughter. The daughter I never knew I had. I saw her at Heathrow. She's...she's the image of her mother. I knew her...her mother...so many years ago. Long before I knew Demetria. When I saw Janine I thought I was seeing Louise—her mother. It was uncanny—the likeness. I had to speak to her—we got talking. And then—' His voice broke with emotion. 'I realised...the dates fit—everything fits. Nine months before Janine was born I had an affair with Louise, her mother. Louise never told me—I never knew that she was pregnant with my child. I never knew I had a daughter. Until now.'

Nikos was still. Completely still. In his cheek a muscle worked.

'Your daughter? You're telling me that Janine is your daughter?'

His voice was flat. Disbelieving.

Janine spoke in a low, faint voice. She felt sick, ill.

'You said you knew. You said you knew about Stephanos and me.'

Nikos turned his head. Janine was hanging on to the edge of the table as if it was the only thing that was keeping her upright.

'I knew you were his mistress.' His voice still had that same flat, dead tone.

'Oh, God!' Janine choked, covering her mouth with her hand. 'How could you think such a thing?'

'Very easily,' he replied. There was a grimness now when he spoke. 'My sister told me. How should I doubt her?'

Janine lifted her eyes to him. He was still the same man she had embraced so short a time ago.

But he was a totally different man.

One she had never known.

'All along…' Her voice was a thread. 'You thought I was Stephanos's… Stephanos's…' The word choked her. 'His mistress—'

She felt the pressure building up in her, up and up, unbearably.

'Oh, God! Oh, God!' Her hand flew to her mouth again and she lurched away from the table.

With wide, distraught eyes, she stared for a moment at the hideous tableau in front of her.

'Janine! My dearest child! *Pethi mou!*' Stephanos held out his hands to her.

She ignored them. Slowly, as if she were drowning, she shook her head from side to side. Then, with a cry of anguish, she ran indoors, to gain the blessed, solitary sanctuary of the bathroom.

*   *   *

The world heaved around her. Heaved, inverted, turned the wrong way up. It was like some hideous jumbled nightmare, where the floors became ceilings, the ceilings floors.

And there was no way out—none. No way to wake and find it all a horrible, terrible nightmare.

She felt sick—so nauseous that she longed for the ability to purge herself.

Purge every last day and night of this vile, hideous nightmare.

The scene on the terrace replayed itself over and over, churning through her in cold, sickening waves. She sat on the floor, on the cold marble tiles, backed into a corner as if she could bury herself in the wall. Her hands were pressed over her mouth, her knees hunched to her chest.

She was shivering—shivering with shock, and horror, and disbelief.

But believe it she must. She had no choice. Out there on the terrace two realities had crashed into each other, and she had been sucked, as if down into a vortex, into that other vile reality that Nikos Kiriakis inhabited.

She gagged in her throat.

He thought she had been Stephanos's mistress. Had thought it all along. From the moment he had laid eyes on her—from before then. And he had believed it right until the truth had been forced in front of his disbelieving eyes.

He had not wanted to believe the truth. Had wanted—*wanted*—to stick with his own sickening reality—that she was Stephanos's mistress.

Stephanos's mistress—

The vile words stabbed at her again.

That was what he thought her.

A married man's mistress. His sister's husband's mistress…

Shock buckled through her again.

Shock upon shock.

He was Demetria's brother. Nikos Kiriakis was Stephanos's brother-in-law.

And a man on a mission. A mission to get rid of the threat to his sister's marriage. By a method that could not fail. By seducing Stephanos's mistress away from him.

And that was exactly what he'd done. Calculatingly, deliberately, cold-bloodedly.

He'd come to the hotel with no other purpose than to seek her out—and seduce her.

She lifted her head, lowering her hands. She had to face up to this. Had to.

She said the words. Said them clear and incontestably.

'Nikos Kiriakis seduced me deliberately. He thought I was Stephanos's mistress. There was no other reason he had an affair with me.'

It was like a knife going into her. A knife so deep she gasped aloud with the pain of it.

'And that means that everything—everything that ever happened between us—was a lie. Everything.'

She said the words. Took them into her. Squeezed them tight to wring every last drop from them. Every last pain.

Everything.

Even that most precious moment of all just now, before her dreams had been destroyed before her eyes, that precious moment when for a few brief seconds she had believed, had actually believed, that Nikos had asked her to marry him...

Her face buckled again as the agony of it knifed through and through her, again and again.

There were voices in the bedroom beyond. Shouting, yelling. In Greek. One was Stephanos's—his gruff tones dominated, excoriating in their fury. The other voice was lower—biting out in terse, grim tones. She could understand not a word of what was said. There was a final volley of fury, one last grim reply. Then she heard footsteps, heavy, receding. Then silence.

There came a low, urgent rapping on the bathroom door.

'Janine!' It was Stephanos.

She made no reply.

'Janine—my child—my dearest girl—I must speak to you! I must! Come out, please!'

She could hear the emotion in her father's voice.

Her father.

All her life she had wondered about her father, questioned her mother and got no answers. None.

'Oh, darling, don't ask! It's all so long ago.' That was all she had ever had got out of her mother. At first she had grown up thinking there was something terrible about her father—or that she did not deserve to have one. Then, eventually, as she had come to understand her mother's lifestyle—the endless parade of men, the endless houses they'd gone to live in, apartments they'd occupied for a brief time, nothing more, the ceaseless restlessness of her mother, her pointless, idle, butterfly existence—she had arrived at a bitter conclusion. Her mother had simply had no idea which of her lovers had fathered her.

Sometimes, when she was an adolescent, on holiday from the boarding school she'd been packed off to as soon as her mother could get away with it, she had searched the faces of her mother's myriad acquaintances, trying to see if there was any resemblance to herself in them.

But how could she have seen any when she herself was the image of her own mother? Only her brown eyes were a clue—and hardly a helpful one. Her mother had seldom fallen for blonds.

So slowly, bitterly, she had come to accept that she would never know who her father was, or what nationality, or even if he was still alive.

Until a chance encounter—whose statistical improbability still made her feel terrified at how easy it would have been for it never to have taken place—had changed her life for ever.

The moment was engraved on her memory. She, arriving back in London, heading down to Baggage Reclaim, had seen a man pause by the entrance to the first-class lounge, pause and stare, as if he were seeing a ghost.

She might have taken no notice, intent on collecting her luggage, had the man not said, in a stunned, disbelieving voice, 'Louise?'

He'd put a hand out, saying something in a language she had not at first recognised, and repeated her mother's name. She'd stopped then.

She knew that her physical resemblance to her mother sometimes caused confusion, and this man was about the right age to have known her. And since he was clearly a habitué of first-class lounges, looked to be wearing a hand-tailored suit and was, moreover, good-looking with silvering hair, he was just the type.

She'd shaken her head, pausing fleetingly. 'No, I'm Louise's daughter.' She'd spoken in English, knowing that, despite his clearly non-English appearance, a cosmopolitan man like him would be bound to speak it himself.

'Ah, yes,' he answered. 'Even Louise, with her incredible beauty, could not have defied time so much!'

He rested his eyes on her. They were kind eyes, she thought, and just a touch familiar somehow. She wondered at it. Had she ever met him before?

'And you have very clearly inherited her beauty—I hope you will not mind my saying so?'

She smiled back. 'Not at all.'

He nodded, and then said, as if it were something he ought to say, 'And how is Louise these days? If you are her daughter, then she must have married at some point. She was very against marriage when I knew her!'

Her face stilled. 'Louise died three years ago. A car crash.'

His sympathy was immediate. 'I'm sorry. Please accept my condolences. And to your father.'

She gave a little shake of her head. 'Louise never did marry—her aversion to the institution remained to the end.'

The man looked very slightly shocked, then he looked rueful. 'I remember her being very vehement on the subject, but I put it down to her youth. She was very young—so was I, for that matter! It must have been—' he visibly cast his mind back '—oh, twenty-six years ago now. I remember I met her at the Monaco Grand Prix, so it must have been May. We were together six weeks. She... What is the English expression? She bowled me over! Quite the most beautiful woman I'd ever—'

He stopped. She'd taken a sharp inhalation of breath.

'What is it?' the man asked immediately, concern in his voice.

She stared at him, spoke before she could halt the words, forming them even as her brain registered what he'd just said.

'I'm twenty-five,' she blurted. 'My birthday is in February.'

For a moment he just looked at her, nonplussed. Then, his expression still arrested, he said something in his own language. Staccato. Shocked.

It's Greek, she registered finally. He's Greek.

And he could be... He could be...my...my...

She went on staring at him, her face draining. How often—how often in the night over the years—had she lain awake trying to work out when she must have been conceived? May was right on the button. May, twenty-six years ago...

Her fingers pressed against her lips, the unimaginable thought leaping in her brain. For one long, endless moment she still stared at this foreign, middle-aged stranger. Who had had an affair with her mother the month she must have been conceived.

No! This was insane, absurd! She turned away, almost stumbling.

His arm shot out, strong and halting.

'Wait!' He turned her back towards him. 'Wait,' he said again.

His eyes were searching her face. Then, abruptly, he spoke.

'Who is your father?'

She shook her head. 'I…I don't know.'

Her voice was thin. As shocked as his.

'My mother…my mother never told me. I…I don't think she knew…'

A look of total grimness possessed the man's face.

'Oh, she did! I think she did indeed! I might only have been a temporary *affaire* to her, but while I was her lover she had no one else! I would not share her with anyone!'

Suddenly his expression changed. He looked at her—and she could see the shock in his eyes. More than shock. Suddenly, like a blow, she realised why it was he seemed familiar. It was his eyes. They were darker than hers—but they were hers.

And he was seeing the same in her face.

'I think…' he said, and there was something very strange in his voice—something that gave her the strangest feeling in the world. 'I think we need to talk.'

And that was all it had taken. All it had taken for Stephanos to accept her as his daughter. The daughter he'd never even known he had. He'd demanded no other proof from her, accepted her completely, taken her into his heart, his life, without question, without doubt. With strong and immediate love.

But with miracles there came a price, and it was one that Janine had known she would pay, and had not begrudged a penny of it. He'd been flying back to Athens because his wife was due to go into hospital and finally be medically investigated for the cause of her long infertility.

She had understood completely, and without resentment, that Stephanos had felt he could not present her as his daughter at such a moment. It would have been too cruel to Demetria to parade a daughter in front of her when she was trying so desperately to give him a child of her own. So she had accepted what had to happen—that she had to remain, for now, a secret, hidden part of his life.

But not as secret as he'd thought...

The low, urgent rapping came again, and her father's voice called, anxiety and concern twisting in his words.

'Janine—please—Please, I have to talk to you. Please—'

Slowly, very slowly, feeling as if death had washed through her and left her a living corpse, she got to her feet. The tie of her robe was almost undone, revealing half her body. With a deathly shudder she refastened it.

Then she went out to face her father—the man Nikos had thought her lover and taken such ruthless steps to part her from.

Stephanos stood uncertainly, a little way back. He looked old, Janine thought, stricken. Her heart went out to him.

'Janine—' His voiced sounded broken. 'I'm so sorry...so sorry.'

A choke sounded in her throat, and then, in a strangled whisper, she said, 'Vava—'

He opened his arms.

'Ela—'

With a heartbreaking cry, she threw herself into his paternal embrace.

He let her cry. Let her cry and cry and cry.

It was ludicrous, she thought, somewhere in the middle of all her tears, ludicrous to be like this. She was a twenty-five-year-old woman, not a little girl, and her life had taken her to places she would not wish on her worst enemy. Yet she felt like a child again. A child being comforted by her father.

He held her wrapped around him, his hands gently patting her back, speaking to her comfortingly in the language she had grown up not even knowing was her birthright.

Gradually, very gradually, the storm of weeping abated. Gradually, very gradually, her father eased her from him. He stroked her hair.

'If I could undo what has happened to you I would give my life's blood,' he told her, and the pain in his voice was terrible to hear. 'I will bear the guilt of this for ever.'

She shook her head, the pain dulled to a heavy ache. 'It wasn't your fault. It wasn't your fault.' She shuddered. 'I should never have…never have…'

She halted suddenly and looked around, fearful.

'Where—where is—?' She stopped, unable to say his name.

'Gone.' Her father's voice was tight. 'He didn't need me to tell him to get out! He's taken off in that cruiser of his.' His voice softened. 'Get your things, my child—we are leaving too.'

She wiped away the last of her drying tears, taking a breath. 'I'll get dressed. Then I'll pack. Am I…am I going back to the hotel?'

There was a tremor in her voice. She didn't want to go there—not ever again.

'No. You are coming to Athens. With me.' Stephanos's voice was decisive.

Janine looked at him. 'But I thought…Demetria?'

She said the name of her father's wife, for whose sake she had accepted that she could not be openly acknowledged as Stephanos's daughter.

'I cannot do it to her,' he had told her, and she had accepted it. 'For ten long, agonising years Demetria has hoped against hope that she will be able to give me the child she knows I long for. I cannot…*cannot*…tell her that I already have a child…she would be devastated. Think herself useless. Already she punishes herself endlessly! Calls herself barren!'

Janine's heart had gone out to her father's wife. She already knew the story of her unhappy first marriage, so she had accepted that, for the time being at least, her existence would have to be kept secret from Demetria.

And because of that...

Her mind veered away. No. She would not let herself think, feel what that secrecy had caused—

Stephanos's face tensed. Taut with guilt.

'I will have to be honest with Demetria. I thought I could keep you hidden entirely from her. That she would never know about you—at least, not until—until...' He took a deep breath. 'Until we might be blessed with a child of our own! Had I thought...for an instant that she might discover your existence and make...' He sighed heavily. '...such an appalling assumption, I would never, never have taken the risk!'

His expression became bleak. 'But now I must try and undo the harm my silence has caused. To my wife—and my daughter.'

He turned to go. 'I will leave you to your packing. Let me know when you are ready, and we can go. Forgive me, but I must phone Demetria. She has no idea I am here. When I called the hotel yesterday, after landing from New York, and was told you had left, I was scared. As soon as I had tracked you down I flew here. I cannot cause Demetria any more anxiety than I have already.'

He bowed his head and left the room. Alone, Janine got on with the bleak, numbing task of packing.

The helicopter flew them back to Skarios airport, and there the executive jet that Stephanos had chartered was ready for takeoff.

As Janine had emerged, finally, from the villa, numb from head to toe, the dazzling view of sea and sky had nearly undone her. Biting hard on her lip, she'd turned her back and walked up the stone steps to the helipad on the flat land above the villa. The rotors had churned idly. All around, the wild landscape had stretched beneath the azure sky.

As they had taken off she'd looked down. The villa had fallen away from them—the terraces and the spectacular pool, the white limestone cliffs and the tiny crescent beach with its little stone quay. No cruiser moored there. Gone.

Gone, gone, gone.

She had shut her eyes, feeling sick.

The flight to Athens took scarcely an hour. A haze of smog sat over the city in the summer heat. Janine sat in the chauffeured car, still feeling numb.

The numbness lasted all the way to the quiet suburb of Kifissia, where the rich of Athens lived, through the security gates of Stephanos's villa, and into the house itself. Servants greeted her father's arrival, not even blinking as he arrived with a beautiful young blonde, ushering her protectingly inside.

Stephanos's face was drawn as he turned to speak to her.

'I must see Demetria,' he said quietly. He gestured to one of the staff, waiting discreetly in the background. 'Will you show *Kyria* Fareham to her room?'

She was taken upstairs, to what was obviously one of the guest suites. It was beautifully furnished. A maid came up to unpack for her. Janine almost told her not to bother. She could not stay here. She could not stay in Greece. She must go—go.

Back to London. Back to work. She could see Stephanos when he came to England. It would be enough. It would have to be.

Her throat tightened dangerously. She went to stand by the window, looking down into the gardens. They were immaculately kept.

The maid closed the closet doors, murmured something, and left. The room was very quiet.

I'm going to have to think about it, she thought. I'm going to have to think about what happened.

I'm going to have to think about Nikos.

Her throat constricted. Her nails clenched in the palm of her hands.

Nikos. Nikos Kiriakis.

Her father's wife's brother.

Well, you always did tell yourself it was a bad idea to fall for him. And it certainly was. Oh, it certainly was.

The enormity of what he had thought swept over her again.

How could I not have noticed? Her question was savage. How could I not have noticed that he thought I was Stephanos's mistress?

The answer was even more savage. Because he thought you already knew you were!

She was back in the nightmare again, the one where everything shifted round, and floors became ceilings, and up became down. She tried to make sense of it—terrible sense of terrible things.

It was, after all, once you had turned the floor to the ceiling, very simple.

He thought you were Stephanos's mistress. That's why he seduced you. To take you away from Stephanos. So you wouldn't threaten his marriage any more. So he started an affair with you himself.

And if Stephanos hadn't come storming down out of the sky, looking for his missing daughter, what then? What would have happened?

Her nails dug into her palms. She heard his voice, soft in her ear. The devil's voice.

I don't want to part with you, Janine. I want us to be together. I want to take you back to Athens with me and make you mine. Recognised by all the world as mine.

Pain lacerated her, and she swayed with it.

A few short hours ago and those words had opened the door of heaven for her.

Now they ushered her to the mouth of hell.

She wrapped her arms around herself to stanch the pain.

A soft knock sounded on the door. She stiffened. The door opened and Janine turned, arms still wrapped around herself.

A woman stood uncertainly in the doorway. She was thin, very thin, but she was beautifully dressed, with the kind of effortless elegance that Janine was used to seeing in wealthy women in the South of France. She looked to be about fifteen years older than Janine.

'May—may I come in?'

The woman's diffidence was painful to see. Slowly Janine nodded.

'This…this is your house,' she answered. Her eyes were riveted on the other woman's face. Her features were strained, and yet Janine could see the stamp that Kiriakis blood had made on them. She felt the knife stab at her again.

The woman closed the door behind her and advanced a little way across the thick carpet. She held out a hand. 'I am Demetria Ephandrou. Stephanos has told me the truth about you. I…I wish we could have met under happier circumstances.'

Janine swallowed. 'Whatever you think of Stephanos now, he never meant you to know about my existence. He knew it would hurt you too much.'

A strange look passed over Demetria's face. 'Hurt me? How could it hurt me?'

'Because…because… To flaunt me in your face, your husband's daughter. When you…when you could not bear a child yourself…'

There was a little choking sound from Demetria. 'So he thought it better that I should believe he had taken a mistress?'

Janine clenched her hands. 'He didn't want you to know anything at all!'

Abruptly, Demetria lifted her hands 'Did he really think his own wife wouldn't tell that something was going on? Did he really think I wouldn't *notice*?' She came forward further. 'Did he think I would rather believe he was unfaithful to me?' Her expression changing, she reached out her hands to Janine again. 'And instead he was hiding a secret I would have rejoiced at learning!'

Janine stared. 'Rejoiced?'

Demetria slipped Janine's nerveless fingers into her own. 'Don't you see?' she said, and there was a crack in her voice. 'You are living proof that Stephanos can father a child. I was frightened, so frightened, that it might be him, not me, who was infertile. Oh, I know the doctors did their tests—but tests can go wrong, can be misleading, give false hope. But to see you here, strong and well and so very, very alive! Stephanos's child!'

Janine looked into Demetria's shining eyes. 'You're *glad* to know about me?'

The world was turning on its head again.

'How can I not be? How can I not be glad that Stephanos has found you after all these years?' She gave a poignant smile that suddenly lit her thin face with beauty. 'It will not stop me moving heaven and earth to give him a child myself, but knowing that he is already a father gives me more hope than ever!'

The smile faded. She let Janine's hands fall. 'I should have had faith in Stephanos. I should have trusted him. He has loved me so faithfully for so many years—even when I was most unhappy, trapped in a loveless marriage. How could I think that he would betray me? And because I did think that, what has happened now is my fault. All my fault!'

Her eyes lifted to Janine, filled with remorse. 'I sent my brother after you. I turned to him because I was desperate and terrified. I do not ask you to forgive me—' Her voice broke off.

Janine's hands twisted. What could she say? Demetria had acted to save her marriage. And so had Nikos. Her throat thickened. It was like some ghastly Greek tragedy— one misunderstanding, one error, bringing with it a wealth of destruction...

'It's...it's all right,' she got out. 'Please—'

She took a constricted breath. She could not take much more of this. The situation was impossible. *Impossible.*

'Do you think,' she went on, speaking jerkily, 'it might be possible for me to lie down for a little while? I feel... I feel...'

Immediately Demetria was all concern. She hurried to the bed, drawing down the damask cover.

'I will send up coffee. Or do you prefer tea? Something to eat?'

Janine shook her head. 'Thank you, no. I just need to rest a little.'

Demetria nodded. 'Of course. I...I will leave you, then. For now.'

Face still troubled, she took her leave.

Slowly, Janine sat down on the bed.

Her head was swimming. She let her body fold down onto the bed, lifting up her legs. They felt very heavy. Her whole body felt heavy, numb. Her eyes closed. The cotton pillowcase was cool on her cheek. She reached to pull the damask coverlet back over her.

I want to sleep, she thought. Sleep, but not to dream...

She dreamt. Instantly, immediately.

She was there, at the villa, on the terrace. Nikos was beside her, his arm around her. She leant into him, feeling his strength, his solidity. Joy filled her. Joy and relief. She had had such a terrible nightmare, but now she had woken from it. A nightmare so awful she did not want to think about it. But it was over. She was here, with Nikos, and he was holding her and everything was wonderful and beautiful and blissful…

He was making love to her, moving over her body, whispering to her, murmuring, his hands gliding over her skin, his mouth caressing her… She was on fire, on sweet fire, her limbs dissolving. The fire was burning through her, and through him, and she cried out, cried out…

Her eyes flew open.

To an empty room.

Misery enfolded her, wrapping around her like weed, drowning her.

She curled in on herself against the misery, against the pain lancing and lancing through her.

It was a lie—everything was a lie! I meant nothing to him, nothing. Less than nothing—I was just something to be picked up, manipulated, and disposed of. Whatever it took. A problem to be sorted. A threat to be disarmed, demolished, removed.

And what had it taken? A look, a day, a kiss, a smile. She had gone down at the first fence, willingly going with him, putting up not the slightest resistance. She had melted at his feet.

He didn't have to break a sweat to seduce me…

A chill went through her. Demetria had known what she was doing when she sent Nikos to deal with her…

She had sent a master to do the job. The job of seducing the woman she thought was stealing her husband.

Except that I wasn't that woman. I was just—

What was the word the military used? When unintended targets got hit?

Collateral damage.

That was what she had been. Collateral damage.

The target hadn't existed at all.

Her stomach iced.

But the damage was real.

Horribly, horribly real.

She gave a smothered cry, flinging back her arm across the pillow, staring up at the ceiling with wide, pained eyes.

CHAPTER SEVEN

SHE dined that night with Stephanos and Demetria. The strain was all but unbearable. It was an awkward, painful meal, and Janine could hardly eat. The delicious food tasted like straw. Conversation was minimal, stilted. They talked only of innocuous things, like the weather and the wedding they'd been to on Long Island.

What made it worse was that it should have been a joyful meal, thought Janine anguishedly. After all Stephanos's fears Demetria had accepted her; she would have a recognised place in her father's family. She could be her father's daughter for all the world to see. She could love him openly, freely. Without hiding or secrecy or worry about hurting Demetria. She should be glad, rejoicing. And so she would have been...

She would have to go, she knew. She could not stay here, however much she wanted to spend precious time with Stephanos, get to know him, the father she had never known. The father she had never been told about.

Demetria found it very hard to accept Louise's actions.

'How could she not have told Stephanos she was pregnant?' she asked uncomprehendingly.

'I think Louise simply didn't want any hassle,' Janine answered. 'She must have known Stephanos would insist on marrying her. And she would have refused—she always hated the idea of marriage. She saw it as a shackle for women. Constricting their freedom. So she never told him, just went ahead and had me.'

She didn't look at Stephanos as she spoke, but she could feel his pain—because it was her pain too. Her mother had denied them both the chance to know each other, love each other.

'And yet,' she said, saying what must be said, 'if it had been otherwise then Stephanos would have married Louise, and not you.'

Pain went through Demetria's eyes.

'Stephanos would have had a child,' she said in a low, anguished voice.

'I want only you, Demetria! With or without children, I want only you!'

Her husband caught her hand, holding it hard. Between them, tangible in its power, Janine could sense the strength of their love, holding them together against their mutual grief. What must it be like, she thought, to be loved like that?

No! Don't think, don't think!

Instead she awknowledged the painful irony that she should have been born to a woman with so few maternal feelings when Demetria yearned for a child with all her being. She found herself giving a small prayer that her father's wife should be granted the blessing she so longed for.

She has a generous heart, thought Janine. She could so easily have bitterly resented my existence, and instead she has welcomed it, rejoiced in it. Yes, perhaps there is an element of what she told me, that I am proof that Stephanos can father a child, but for all that she could so easily have seen me as a taunt to her own infertility.

She felt a silent shiver go through her. Had Stephanos only realised how large Demetria's heart was then he would never have thought to keep his new-found daughter's existence a secret—arousing his wife's suspicions and making her act so swiftly, so devastatingly, to protect her marriage…

Misery filled her. None of this would have happened. This vile, sick situation would never have arisen.

Another thought pierced her, even more anguished.

Supposing Stephanos had introduced her into his family life straight away, the moment they arrived in Greece? Supposing she had come here, to his own house, had met Demetria—and her brother? An image leapt in her mind so painful she could not bear it—Nikos coming here, Demetria's brother, being introduced to his brother-in-law's long-lost daughter, knowing who she really was right from the beginning…

She saw him as vividly as if he had been real, looking at her with those night-dark eyes, taking her hand, welcoming her—

The beeping of the house phone sounded and she blinked. Nikos was gone.

Well, that much was true. Nikos was gone. Gone from her life for ever. And she must go too. She could never meet him again. *Never.*

And she didn't want to see him. The very thought of him made her buckle with nausea. After what he had done to her…

The instinct to run, run and lick her wounds, was overpowering.

Tomorrow. I'll go tomorrow. After breakfast. I must find out about flights and all that. She would ask her father as soon as he'd finished speaking on the phone.

He'd answered in Greek, his face tightening slightly, then nodded, said something more in Greek, and hung up.

She opened her mouth to speak, but her father forestalled her.

'Janine—will you come with me a moment, *pethi mou*?'

There was tension in his voice; she could hear it.

He got to his feet and waited for her to do likewise. Puzzled, she did so. The atmosphere seemed strained somehow—and yet expectant.

She saw Demetria look at her, then glance to meet her husband's eye in silent communication. The look in the other woman's eyes was tense as well. Then she got to her feet too and came across to Janine. She took her hands in hers.

'I caused you great harm,' she told her. 'I never meant to, but I did. The harm cannot be undone—but what can be done will be done.' She leant forward to place a kiss on each of Janine's cheeks.

Janine's eyes widened. The moment seemed so solemn suddenly. Then, just as suddenly, Demetria's face suddenly lit. 'Yet I am happy as well as sad—I cannot help it!' Her hands squeezed Janine's. 'You do not know how much I have longed for this day! Oh, it should not have been like this, I know—but all the same I cannot stop my happiness! And that it should be you of all people fills my heart with joy!'

Janine just stared at her. Demetria's words were inexplicable.

Then her father was touching her shoulder, drawing her away. He said something to Demetria, and she nodded. The tension was back in the room, yet Demetria's face still was lit from within.

Bemused, Janine went meekly with her father. Perhaps she needed to sign documents or something—to do with the transfer of money he was making over to her.

They went out of the large, ornate salon, across the wide marbled hallway to a door set off a small lobby towards the rear of the huge house. Janine could hear her footsteps echo off the marble floor.

Stephanos went ahead of her and opened the door. She stepped through into the room beyond.

And stopped dead.

Nikos was inside.

Blindly, instinctively, she turned to run, bolt, flee. But her father was there, catching her shoulders.

'My child, my child—I know, I know. But this must be done. It must.'

There was grimness beneath the softness, the sympathy. Gently but inexorably he turned her around, ushering her forward a little so he could close the door behind him.

She wanted to shut her eyes, wanted to cover her face, but she could not. Nikos was standing there, across the room. It was a kind of study, she noticed with the tiny fragment of her brain that was still registering the existence of anything that was not Nikos. There was a large desk, a computer on it, leather chairs, shelves with books, massive tomes and business journals. A masculine place. A place of business and financial transaction, of legal documents, contracts and commerce.

Nikos looked completely at home in it.

He was wearing a suit. Dark this time, not the lightweight suit she'd first laid eyes on him in. Whereas in the light grey suit he'd looked elegant and devastating, now he looked sombre.

And just as devastating.

That was the worst thing, she thought, as her mind fragmented into a thousand shards, each one needle-sharp, piercing her flesh like knives. That she could feel her heart jolt as her eyes took him in, took in those broad shoulders, the long, lean body, that beautifully planed and sculpted face, those dark gold-flecked eyes.

Veiled eyes.

Eyes that saw her but did not look at her.

Eyes that were shuttered, had no expression in them.

Her nails dug into the palms of her hands. As they did so she saw that a muscle was working in his cheek. He looked grim, and tense.

Why? Why was Stephanos doing this to her? Why this hideous ordeal? How could he be so cruel to her?

The silence stretched endlessly, it seemed. But it could

only have been a few seconds—though they seemed to last for ever, Janine felt.

Stephanos spoke. Though she could understand none of the words, Janine could hear the heaviness in them. As he spoke Nikos's face tensed even more. His eyes moved from her to look at her father.

Then, abruptly, as Stephanos fell silent, they snapped back to her.

For a second something blazed in them, something that made her flinch with shock. Then it was gone. The veil was back over those dark and gold eyes, a veil she could not see past.

Stephanos placed a hand on her shoulder, turning her slightly towards him.

'My daughter.' His voice was solemn now, as Demetria's had been. 'Great wrong has been done to you. Now it shall be righted.' He placed his other hand upon her other shoulder, leant forward and dropped a kiss upon her forehead. It was almost like a ritual, a paternal blessing.

Then, exchanging one long last, level look with Nikos, he left the room.

She wanted to run, bolt, flee from the room. But her feet were rooted to the ground, her body frozen.

Nikos looked at her. As before, the moment seemed to last for all eternity, not the few fleeting seconds that was all its true duration.

Her nails dug deeper into the palms of her hands.

What was he going to say? What could he say?

That he'd made a mistake? An error?

Collateral damage.

The chill euphemism echoed in her mind.

She looked at the man who up until this moment had never set eyes on her without thinking that she was a woman who had taken the financial protection of a married man—a rich, married man—a man—and the irony of it bit so deep she had to stop herself crying out—a man old enough to be her father.

For one long, ghastly moment he went on looking at her, not speaking. Then, abruptly, his voice broke the unendurable silence between them.

'Janine—'

Just her name. The softness of his pronunciation, the familiarity, undid her. Her nails seemed to pierce her skin, so deep did she dig them into her palms. For one terrifying moment she felt she was going to burst into tears, sob with pain and despair, break down entirely.

She wouldn't do it. She would *not*. She would not break down. For some horrible reason her father thought she should endure the ordeal of facing Nikos again—why, she could not tell. She didn't want an apology, didn't want an expression of regret, didn't want any awkward, stilted voicing of contrition.

With immense effort she schooled herself.

'Yes?' Her voice was cool, unemotional.

Something flashed in his eyes. For a moment she thought it was anger. But that could not be. It was so totally inappropriate that she must have imagined it.

'This is a difficult situation for us both,' he said tightly. 'Let us try and get through it with as much grace as we can muster.'

He looked, she thought suddenly, very formidable. Every inch a man of wealth and consequence, a man born to riches, a powerful man. Like a shot to the heart she remembered that first frisson she had felt as he towered over her in his business suit at the poolside, making her feel so exposed, so vulnerable in her skimpy bikini.

No, she mustn't remember that. Mustn't remember anything as dangerous as that.

He was speaking again.

'The arrangements have been set in motion. From my meeting with Stephanos this afternoon I understand that he has already taken steps to settle an appropriate sum on you, as capital. That will, of course, remain yours. He and I have also agreed a separate sum, from my own resources, that will be settled on you as income. As for the ceremony itself, I know that Demetria is very keen to make a splendid occasion of it. Whether you are happy with that, or would prefer something quieter, I leave entirely to you. Whichever you choose, you will, of course, have my support—whatever Demetria's feelings on the subject.'

He spoke briskly, as if running through the key points of a business deal. As he finished he looked at her questioningly, as if affording her the opportunity to input her comments, if any, before he moved on.

She stared at him blankly.

'I haven't the faintest idea what you're talking about,' she said.

A frown creased between his eyes.

'I appreciate, Janine, that your background means you are unfamiliar with the concept of settlements and the disposition of property on such an occasion, but be assured that Stephanos is obviously ensuring that your interests are safeguarded to the utmost. You may safely leave everything to him. As for the other matter...' His voice became dry. 'You may, if you prefer, leave that equally safely to Demetria. She will, I know, be in her element.' His mouth tightened minutely. 'It is, after all, something she has longed for on my behalf.'

'What is?' She was lost—completely lost. Nikos looked at her.

'To see me married,' he said tightly.

She drew her breath sharply. It was like a blow coming out of the blue. And it hurt. Over everything that had happened, all her pain and misery, this smote at her with lethal force.

'You're getting married?' Her voice was faint. Her nails spasmed in her palms.

He was looking at her as if she was deranged.

'Have you not listened to anything I have told you?' he demanded. He could have been speaking to an underling, a recalcitrant employee. 'Stephanos and I have agreed the settlement—you are, it goes without saying, extremely well provided for. Demetria will undertake the organisation of whatever form of ceremony you prefer. Unless you feel strongly, I would suggest a civil ceremony—but of course if you wish I can arrange for you to receive whatever instruction is necessary so that you may participate in an Orthodox service. Our wedding can be as large or as small, as public or private as you wish. Demetria will make all the arrangements necessary.'

Faintness was washing through her. Faintness and disbelief.

'Our wedding...'

Her voice trailed off.

He took a step forward. 'Our wedding,' he repeated. He took a breath. 'Janine, we must be married. It is obvious. Surely you understand that?' There was tension suddenly in his voice.

Slowly, her head shook from side to side.

'No. I don't understand.' Her voice was still faint.

Something changed in his eyes. And in his voice.

'Don't you?'

She felt her breath catch. There was a caress in his words as tangible as if he had stroked her arm.

Pain squeezed through her.

'Don't you, Janine?'

He reached towards her. The gold in his eyes was molten suddenly.

She backed away. Blocking. Rejecting.

'No! I don't understand.' Her voice was hectic. 'I don't understand in the slightest! It's ridiculous, absurd!'

The flash of anger in his eyes came again. 'Try saying that to Stephanos! To Demetria!' His mouth thinned.

'They're consumed with guilt. Each of them feels that this…débâcle…is their fault. Stephanos's for not confiding in Demetria about your existence. And Demetria's—' his voice became grimmer yet '—Demetria's for coming to such a disastrous conclusion about your identity!' His eyes held Janine's. 'Our marriage is the only way they can accept what has happened. The only remedy.'

She shook her head. It felt heavy, muzzy.

'If you love your father as I love my sister then we must do what they so desperately need us to do. Only marriage will recover the situation.' His face tensed even more, and then in a heavy, hard voice he said, 'They feel you have been dishonoured.'

'Dishonoured?' Her voice was incredulous.

That emotion flashed in his eyes again.

'This is Greece, Janine. In Greece a father protects his child. In Greece a family holds together, is the most sacred part of society. Stephanos feels that he has failed to protect you. That his failure has resulted in…what has happened. And Demetria—Demetria is punishing herself for having sent me to…deal with you. For her, for Stephanos, the only way that this…dishonour…can be undone is by our marriage. Then and only then will our families be united once more.'

She looked at him. Looked at him long, and hard. Then, in a brittle, taut voice, she said, 'I have never heard anything so sick in all my life.'

She reached for the door, pulled it open, and walked out.

She crossed the marble hallway. Her footsteps were jerky, her body stiff as a board. She headed for the staircase.

She had not gained the lowest step before the double doors to the drawing room were flung open.

Demetria hurried out.

'So! Is it done?' Her face was alight with hope. It shone

like a beacon from her eyes. But behind the hope Janine could see another emotion.

Guilt. Haunting her eyes, bringing tension to her thin body.

Her father came up behind his wife, his hand at her back. Expectancy was in his face. Guilt shadowing his eyes.

Janine looked from one to the other. A cold, horrible numbness started to creep over her. They meant it. They really meant it. They wanted her and Nikos to marry.

Were desperate for it.

'Janine. *Pethi mou*—'

The anxiety in her father's voice was audible.

'My dear…' Demetria's voice was faltering.

She looked at Demetria, tormented by guilt and by her infertility. Haunted by the damage her unfounded suspicions of her husband had done to his daughter. Looked at her father, who had taken her into his arms, his life, without question, without doubt, with only joy and gratitude. Now tormented by what had happened to her. What his silence had caused.

Footsteps sounded behind her, heavy on the marble floor, issuing from the room she had just bolted from. They approached steadily.

Nikos came to stand at her side.

She stood, frozen, beside him.

She wanted to move, step away from him. But the numbness was spreading all through her. Like heavy, dulling anaesthetic.

Stephanos said something in Greek. Sharp. Enquiring.

Nikos answered. His voice level.

She heard her name—that was all she could make out. Two pairs of eyes flew to her. Her father's and his wife's. Tension radiated from them like cold waves. Numbing her even more.

'Janine?'

It was Nikos. Nikos saying her name. Asking her a question she did not need spelt out.

The numbness reached her brain. She could feel nothing—nothing at all.

Nothing.

Nothing except an inescapable inevitability.

She yielded to what she knew, in her bleak heart of hearts, she had to do.

She bowed her head.

'Yes.'

It was all she said. All she had to say.

Before her eyes, her father's face broke into a smile. Relief shone from him. Demetria's eyes took on the shining look that they had held just before Janine had left the drawing room, so short a while ago. Her father's wife's strange words then made sense now. Horrible, hideous sense.

But it was too late. All too, too late.

Demetria surged forward. She caught Janine's hands, bestowing a kiss on either cheek. Her father came behind her, hugging her. Then Demetria was kissing her brother. Her father's hand was stretching out to Nikos. Slowly, through the numbness that was complete now, Janine saw Nikos hesitate. Then he took Stephanos's hand, clasping it. He said something. Her father nodded. Something was exchanged between them. Between the man whose daughter had been dishonoured, however unintentionally, and the man who was now making due reparation for that dishonouring.

It was like something out of the Middle Ages. Not something that had anything to do with her. It could not be. It could not.

Then Demetria was clapping her hands.

'Champagne! We must have some champagne!' She hurried off eagerly to summon one of her staff.

Stephanos was ushering the happy couple back into the drawing room. His face was wreathed in smiles.

It was a nightmare. As Demetria returned, and a bottle of chilled vintage champagne arrived, Janine could only stand there. The numbness kept her going, kept her upright. Nikos stood beside her.

Stephanos gave her a glass of champagne. She took it in nerveless fingers. Her father gave a toast. She could understand not a word, but it was clearly a toast.

Their glasses were raised.

She drank.

The liquid, chill and effervescent, slipped down her throat.

Just as the champagne had slipped down her throat when Nikos had borne her away on his cruiser to the fate he'd intended for her...

But in her worst nightmares she had never expected this.

Someone else was living in her body. She could tell. It seemed to be moving, walking and talking, and she was smiling. Smiling when her father kissed her, smiling when Demetria chattered away. Smiling when visitors came to call and she was introduced.

'Stephanos's English daughter,' Demetria called her, and whatever people thought they kept it to themselves. 'And my sister-in-law to be!'

There was more astonishment over that announcement than over the unexpected production of Demetria's twenty-five-year-old stepdaughter.

'My dear, you will be envied to death! What *is* your secret? How on earth did you manage to catch our handsome Nikos?'

The enquiry was friendly, but Janine could hear the barb in the voice of this designer-clad matron who was clearly one of Demetria's good friends.

Well, she felt like answering, it was like this...

But even as the vicious thought formed in her mind she

knew that Demetria was rewriting history for public consumption.

'It was a *coup de foudre*!' she exclaimed, clapping her hands as if it really were thundering. 'Janine came out to visit us, and as soon as Nikos set eyes on her he was lost!'

'Wonderful!' cooed her friend. 'But then she is a beauty, and only the most beautiful will do for our handsome, handsome Nikos!'

There was definitely a barb in her voice now.

When she had gone—surely, Demetria said with a gleam in her eyes, to spread the word as fast as possible—her sister-in-law-to-be whispered conspiratorially, 'She wanted an affair with Nikos herself! He turned her down! Mind you…' Her voice became even more conspiratorial '…she was one of the few he did. My darling brother has a reputation that—'

She stopped dead.

'It's all right,' said Janine.

The haunted look was back in Demetria's face. 'It's why I sent him,' she said in a low voice. 'I knew if anyone could entice a woman away from another man it would be Nikos.' Guilt resonated in her voice.

'It's all right,' said Janine again. What else could she say?

She was moving in a daze, a haze of numbness. She had no will left of her own.

Apart from introducing her as her sister-in-law-to-be to all her extensive social acquaintance, Demetria was whisking her around the most expensive shops in Kolonaki, the chic shopping district of Athens. Money burned through her fingers in amounts that Janine could not bear to watch. At first she tried to stop her, but Demetria didn't listen. And she didn't listen when Janine said she did not want a religious wedding.

'I know it will seem strange to you, but you are Greek—

you are Stephanos's daughter—and to be Greek is to be Orthodox—' Demetria began.

But Janine held fast. She might let Demetria go crazy in clothes shops, but she would not make a mockery of religion—any religion—with this travesty she was engaged upon.

But she must not think about that. Must not think about what she was doing. She must not. Or she might break down and shatter.

And she must not do that. Stephanos and Demetria needed to see her married. She had to go through with it. She had to.

Her feelings didn't matter.

Besides, she had none. She was quite, quite numb.

As for Nikos, she never set eyes on him.

It was her only mercy.

'My wretched brother!' Demetria lamented. 'What a time to go haring off to Australia! Business—always business. But—' she sighed '—at least he is getting it all out of the way. He has promised me that you will honeymoon for a month!'

Her eyes gleamed, though there was a brightness in them that was almost desperate, Janine thought. 'And you will have a trousseau to die for!' She glanced at the diamond-studded watch on her wrist, and tut-tutted. 'Oh, we have scarcely time for lunch before your next fitting.' She gave a laugh. There was a feverish note in it. 'How can we possibly get everything done in time?'

The days slipped by, one by one. August slipped into September. The heat hardly slackened. Janine stayed in the air-conditioned interiors, still feeling numb.

Two days before the wedding Nikos returned to Athens.

'He is coming to dinner tonight,' announced Stephanos at breakfast.

Janine's fingers clenched on her cutlery.

Demetria exclaimed volubly at the short notice, but rallied immediately. She spent all day preparing the house. Bouquets arrived, heavy and scented, lavished all over the house. Demetria spent time closeted with her chef. Servants polished the house till it shone. Stephanos, Janine noted, kept to his office in the city.

In mid-afternoon Demetria banished her upstairs. 'Rest, then bathe. I will send Maria to dress you at eight, and the hairdresser and stylist come at half-past seven.'

Numbly, Janine did what she was told.

'Oh, my dear, you look wonderful!'

Demetria clapped her hands together, clasping them to her bosom. She herself looked incredibly slim and elegant in dark blue. Janine was in emerald-green.

The dress was a masterpiece—a couturier number—wrapped around her in tiny overlapping plissé tissue from breasts to ankles. Her shoulders and arms were bare, her hair swept up into a complicated pleat that had taken nearly an hour to dry and style and pin. Her make-up was immaculate—the professional stylist had applied it.

She wore no jewellery. Not a scrap.

'No—nothing,' Demetria had insisted when her maid remonstrated, and had said something in a whisper to Maria that had brought a conspiratorial smile to the older woman's face.

Demetria held up a hand. From downstairs, quite audible, came the sound of the front door admitting someone. Voices murmured.

'I will check on Stephanos,' Demetria said to Janine. 'Five minutes,' she instructed Maria.

The maid nodded, and set about fussing one last time over Janine.

Janine stood staring at her reflection in the long glass.

She did indeed look spectacular. The dress moulded her figure revealingly, but without the slightest trace of vulgarity. She looked what she was supposed to look—the rich daughter of a rich man.

About to marry another rich man.

A man who was marrying her because he had dishonoured her and who had, quite accidentally, taken her for the mistress of a married man...

I can't do this. I can't. I can't go through with it. I can't endure it. I can't face it.

Her breath froze in her throat.

I can't face him.

She felt the numbness start to crack—tiny, filigree cracks that began to radiate out across her consciousness. They spread rapidly, terrifyingly, and underneath was seeping something so painful she could not deny its existence. It forced itself upon her, welling up through every crack...

There was the lightest touch on her hand. Maria was looking at her questioningly.

'*Kyria*, I think it is time to go down now.'

Janine nodded. Walking carefully in her high heels and long dress, she crossed the room and headed down the wide staircase. There was no one in the hall, but she could hear voices in the drawing room.

She swept across the hall and one of the staff opened the double doors for her. She nodded her thanks and walked in.

Stephanos and Demetria were there, already seated. Nikos was standing. He was dressed like Stephanos, in a tuxedo. Janine felt her insides hollow.

As she came in, he turned.

His eyes focused on her with an expression of absolute arrest. He didn't move, not a muscle, just looked at her.

For a moment, a long, terrifying moment, she felt as if she were standing on the very edge of a cliff. As if one single movement of her body would send her hurtling over the precipice to be destroyed on the rocks below.

Then, like a saviour, her father walked up to her and took her hands.

'My beautiful daughter.'

There was such pride in his voice, such love. Such gratitude.

She felt her heart squeeze.

Then Nikos was speaking. His voice was deep. Oppressively formal.

'Janine.'

That was all. Then he was slipping a hand inside the jacket of his tuxedo. He drew out a slim, oblong box.

'Demetria told me you would be wearing green tonight.' He flicked open the box, his voice quite impersonal.

The lamplight made the emeralds within gleam with green fire. Nikos took out the necklace, discarding the case. Taking an end in each hand, he approached Janine.

'Turn around.'

Wordlessly, she turned.

She felt his fingers at her nape. Faintness drummed through her and she fought it off. This was part of the charade. This hollow, meaningless, bitter charade that she had to endure for the sake of her father, who loved her, for Demetria, who loved Stephanos...

His fingertips touched the delicate hairs at the back of her head as he fastened the necklace around her. The stones felt cold to her skin. Then he stepped away, returning to his original position in the room.

His sister gave a little gasp.

'Nik, they are exquisite!' She said something else in Greek. He nodded, glancing at Stephanos. Then he slipped his hand inside his breast pocket again and drew out a smaller jewel case. A ring case, square and bulbous. As before, he flicked it open.

The ring—diamonds set with emeralds—drew another gasp from Demetria. Janine watched in silence, as if she were far outside her body, and waited while he removed the ring, came forward, lifted her nerveless hand and slid the engagement ring on her finger. Then he raised her hand to his lips and kissed it.

He might have been a stranger.

He is a stranger—a man you do not know. You thought you did, but you didn't.

But you've got to marry him all the same...

'Thank you,' she murmured, as a fiancée *should* thank the man who had offered to marry her, to restore the honour lost so accidentally, so unintentionally. Her eyes slid away.

Then one of the staff entered, bearing a tray of champagne.

All through dinner, through each of the long and complicated courses with which Demetria's chef had excelled himself, Janine saw the ring winking on her finger. It seemed to drag her hand down, making it feel heavy, clumsy.

She sat opposite Nikos, letting her eyes constantly slip past him to focus on a painting on the wall of the dining room. It looked like a Dutch landscape. Seventeenth-century. By the end of dinner she was acquainted with the position of every lowering cloud, every sail of the passing barge, every feature of every distant peasant.

What was talked about she had no idea. The evening was a blur. She seemed to pass the time answering questions put to her and sipping from her wine glass. There was a lot of wine. The champagne, then white, then red, and sweet. As she sipped her dessert wine she remembered the bouquet of the Sauternes she had drunk that first lunchtime on the terrace of the villa, hot in the summer sun, with the scent of the dry earth, the heat of the air.

The languor of desire.

Of their own volition her eyes slid to Nikos. She could not help it. She had to look at him. Had to.

She let herself go back. Let time wash her away. Sweep

her back to where she once had been, gazing at the man she had so desired. Possessing him.

Weakness hollowed through her, and an ache so great she felt it fill her every atom. She sat across the table from him and poured out her desire.

He was talking to Stephanos. It was something to do with property and prices, location. She was not paying attention—hadn't been at all. They'd slipped back into Greek, and she welcomed it. Now all she had to do was sit here and give herself to the wonder, the breathtaking wonder, of gazing at him, feeling her heart fill and fill and fill…

Suddenly, without warning, without any pause in what he was saying to her father, Nikos's eyes flicked to hers.

They caught her gaze as a hunter snared game, seizing and holding her so fast she could not even breathe. For the long, timeless moment he held her she could not not move, transfixed by his regard.

The world disappeared. Simply disappeared. Stephanos's voice faded, the softly playing baroque background music faded, Demetria faded, the room faded, blurred. There was nothing left, and no one. No one except Nikos, holding her with his eyes, those dark and gold eyes. Holding her…

Just holding her…

Nikos, holding her…

Then his head turned back to Stephanos and he let her go.

The room surged back around her. There was her father, talking, music playing from the recessed speakers, the wine winking in her glass, the scent of Demetria's perfume, the flowers on the table.

Her heart was beating. Beating so rapidly she felt it racing inside her, pulsing with a strength that made her feel weak.

She reached for her wine again.

Demetria said something and she turned to her, fixing a

polite smile on her face, trying to make her brain work again, function.

She started to talk about something quite innocuous. It might have been flowers. Or food. Janine couldn't really tell. She murmured, and nodded, and smiled politely.

Trying to stop her eyes stealing back to where they yearned to go.

To Nikos.

Who had taken her to heaven. And left her in hell.

CHAPTER EIGHT

FOR a second, as Stephanos drew his attention again and Demetria diverted Janine's, Nikos felt a surge of some powerful emotion he recognised as rage. Rage that he had been interrupted.

He had got her! For the first time since she had run from him, as white as milk, on that gut-twisting morning at the villa, he had got her! She had been responding to him—helplessly, totally. Had they been on their own he would have hesitated not a second—he'd have come around the table, swept her up into her arms and made her his own again!

Frustration seethed through him. She was so incredibly, fantastically beautiful! She'd walked into the room and his breath had simply stopped in his lungs. Never, *never* had she been more beautiful!

Or so untouchable.

Totally untouchable.

But then he'd known that from the moment when, like an icy deluge down his spine, Stephanos's words had sunk in. The girl he'd thought his brother-in-law's mistress was his daughter.

He could still feel now the shock that had buckled through him as the world inverted around him and black had turned to white before his very eyes. The hideous scene in the villa when truth—blazing, self-evident, convincing truth—had dissolved in his hands. And new truth, a truth that had hollowed him out like a knife eviscerating his guts, had stared at him out of Stephanos's eyes.

Janine's eyes.

The two had blurred.

Like something in a nightmare.

And like something in a nightmare his emotions had blazed in total conflict with each other. Horror that he had taken Stephanos's daughter for his mistress. Realisation that that meant Stephanos didn't *have* a mistress—had never had a mistress—that his sister's marriage was not in danger.

And above all, overriding everything, the realisation that Janine had been taken away from him. Janine—the woman he desired beyond anything. Anyone. The woman he had to possess again—*had to*. His whole being was focused on her—on Janine.

Who had been taken away from him—when he wanted her so much, so much.

Taken away and walled up, here in her father's house. And there had been only one way to get to her. Only one.

He hadn't needed the excruciatingly painful interview in Stephanos's office the afternoon he'd got back to Athens, or the even more painful telephone conversation with a sobbing Demetria, to tell him that.

Marriage. Stephanos demanded it. Demetria begged it.

As for Janine—

His face darkened. He had tried to make her see why they must marry—not for their family, but for themselves. She was trying to deny what they had. What they still had. What they would always have. Couldn't she see that?

Well, he thought, she'd seen it now. Seen it blaze in his eyes, just as he'd seen it blaze in her eyes.

He had to get her to accept it. He had to!

Frustration ate at him. Stephanos had all but ordered him to take himself off while Demetria got on with organising his daughter's wedding. He'd had no choice but to agree. Stephanos had made it totally, absolutely clear that Janine was out of his reach. Out of his reach totally until she had his ring on her finger.

Nikos's mouth tightened. He'd accepted Stephanos's edict, had been in no position to object, but every day in

Australia had been a torment. Even tonight he was under stringent scrutiny, forced to behave with a formality towards Janine that was excruciating. He would be allowed no time with her alone. Stephanos had made that clear. No chance to speak to her—no chance to touch her, to break through her denial. No time to break through that wall she had put up around herself.

Slowly he let himself exhale, trying to breathe out the frustration that choked him.

It would not be long now. He had to cling on to that. Soon he would have Janine in bed with him again.

He would count every hour.

Janine closed her eyes and leant her head back against the cool leather headrest. Through her body hummed the low vibration of the twin engines of an executive jet. Her hands rested on the wide leather armrests at either side. On her finger a band of gold glinted.

Her wedding ring.

It was done. It was over. She had married the man who had sought her out to get her into bed with him, out of the bed of the man he had assumed was her rich, married lover.

She heard her own voice echo in her mind, after he'd told her that it was 'obvious' that they must marry—'I have never heard anything so sick in all my life!' But she had gone and done it all the same.

No, she wouldn't think about her wedding. Wouldn't think about marrying Nikos. Wouldn't think about Nikos period.

It was much too dangerous to think about him.

Instead she pulled the numbness back over her, like a blanket, and settled down under its reassuring folds.

'Would you care for something to drink, *Kyria* Kiriakis?'

The soft voice of the flight attendant murmured at her side.

She shook her head. Then promptly changed her mind

and asked for a gin and tonic. She'd drunk no alcohol at all at the opulent reception at one of Athens's top hotels. The champagne in her glass had scarcely touched her lips. She didn't think she could have swallowed. She'd made a pretence of eating, but hadn't been able to force the food down. She'd tried desperately not to look as sick as she'd felt.

The reception had gone on and on, a babble of Greek voices. Everyone had been looking at her, she knew, but she had simply stood there, as tall and immobile as a Greek column, in her ivory satin gown with its narrow skirt and long train. She hoped, for her father's sake and for Demetria's sake, that she had simply looked as if she were suffering from bridal nerves. Certainly she'd been on the receiving end of a few envious looks and remarks from a considerable number of the female guests. She'd smiled a pale smile and said nothing. Feeling numb. Endlessly numb.

Her numbness was a blessed relief.

The only time it had come near to cracking—the way it had that evening when she'd stared at her reflection the night Nikos had come to dinner—had been when they had taken their leave. Her father had taken her in his arms and kissed her on her forehead.

'Remember, my darling girl, that I love you very much.'

That was all he had said, and it had nearly undone her. Then Demetria had been kissing her on both cheeks, clutching at her. Her eyes had been fevered. Janine hadn't been able to bring herself to meet them. For their sakes she had gone through this travesty.

Louise's image floated in front of her eyes. How scornful she would have been! Her daughter's travesty of a marriage would have confirmed all the contempt she had ever felt for the institution.

Her drink arrived and she sipped it. The gin kicked in her throat. She took another sip—more of a gulp this time.

A hand reached over from the seat across the aisle and removed her glass.

'Drinking on an empty stomach is not wise.'

She darted her eyes venomously to where Nikos sat, engrossed in the current issue of the *Harvard Business Review*.

'Give that back!'

He levelled a glance at her.

'You ate almost nothing at the reception. The alcohol will go straight to your head.'

She pulled her eyes away. They had the power to pierce her numbness, and she didn't want that. Her numbness was all that was keeping her going.

She turned her head. Below, the dark mass of the Balkans was relieved only by the occasional gleam of moonlight on a lake or river.

At least it would be cooler in Austria, thought Janine. She had taken no interest whatsoever in the choice of honeymoon destination. She vaguely remembered Demetria asking her whether she liked the Alps, and that was about it.

She went on staring out of the window, seeing nothing.

Across the aisle, Nikos rested his dark eyes on her. The wedding had proved more difficult than he'd anticipated. Demetria must have invited everyone she knew.

He understood why. The wedding had been a statement, a very public statement, that he was making the appropriate reparation to Stephanos's daughter. Only Demetria and Stephanos knew that, of course, which was what had made the wedding so hard. Amongst his male acquaintance there was a general consensus that this was, in effect, a dynastic marriage, drawing the families of Ephandrou and Kiriakis even more closely together. That Stephanos Ephandrou's daughter happened to be a total knockout was considered a bonus for him, whatever the financial advantage and the mutual exchange of corporate cross-holdings that must inevitably be the main commercial driver for the marriage. His female acquaintance had been less generous about his motives.

'Nikos, darling, so you've finally met a woman you've had to marry to get into bed!' one ex-lover had murmured to his face that evening, with a malicious expression in her eyes.

She didn't know it, of course, he thought, as he flicked his eyes over an article on corporate governance, but she'd omitted one vital word from her analysis.

Back.

Back into bed.

That was what his marriage meant to him. The only way to get Janine back in his bed.

The hotel in the beautiful Austrian spa town had once been the summer residence of a Hapsburg prince. Its baroque splendour had been restored to its former glory, and now catered to the most expensive clientele.

Idly, Janine wondered if it was one of her father's.

She walked silently beside Nikos as they were ushered to their suite, and looked about her as she entered. Gilded furniture and heavy drapes made it seem palatial. Their luggage was carried through to the bedroom, and a maid arrived to unpack for them. Janine smiled vaguely at her, avoided looking at the vast four-poster bed, and went into the bathroom, converted from the dressing room it had once been. She locked the door and started to run a bath. The room filled with billowing steam as the huge claw-footed bath began to fill.

With the same numb composure that had got her through since she had gone back to Athens with her father, she took off her suit. It was ivory white, very tight-fitting, and as elegant as it was expensive. She draped it carefully over a gilded chair. Her hair was still in its elaborate coiffeur, and she unpinned it, shaking it loose, then knotting it loosely back up on top of her head. Then she set about removing her make-up. There was an armoury of toiletries supplied at the vanity unit.

When her face had been stripped clean of every last speck of make-up, she took off her underwear and stepped into the bath. She sank into its foaming depths, lying back and gazing up at the ceiling.

She felt tired. Tired all the way through to her bones. A deep, deep exhaustion.

She went on lying in the hot water.

There seemed nothing else to do.

The light above the vanity unit seemed to be pulsing slowly, going in and out of focus. In and out...

After a while, she did not know how long, she got out, dried herself, and wrapped her body in a large bath towel, letting her hair tumble down over her shoulders.

She felt so tired. She needed sleep.

Probably for ever.

The numbness seemed to be wrapping her more tightly.

She walked out of the bathroom into the bedroom.

And stopped dead.

Nikos was getting undressed.

He was down to his shirt and his underpants. His shirt was already open down the front and he was concentrating on slipping off his gold cufflinks.

She stared, transfixed. The tanned, powerful sinews of his thighs drew her eyes inexorably. By effort of will she hauled them away.

It was little improvement. As she raised her gaze it collided head-on with Nikos's. He was sweeping his eyes over her, taking in her tumbled hair, the tightly wound towel around her body, her bare legs and shoulders.

Time seemed to stand still. Then Nikos was strolling towards her and time started again.

He stood in front of her. The expression on his face was

strange—a mix of absolute tension and exultation. He looked down on her, his eyes like powerful searchlights.

'You have absolutely no idea,' he told her slowly, in a deep, throbbing voice, 'none whatsoever, how I have *ached* for this moment...'

His fingers touched her face, just grazing along her cheek.

'*Theos mou*, but you are so beautiful. So beautiful—and mine at last.'

His voice was a husk, low and rasping.

She simply stood there.

This wasn't happening. This couldn't be happening. It couldn't.

'Are you insane?'

The words croaked from her.

But he wasn't listening to her. He was reaching for her, letting his hands slide down her bare arms, then back again, as if he was smoothing lustrous marble.

'Nikos!' Her voice was a faint breath now.

His eyes were half closed. Some emotion seemed to be working in him, powerful, inexorable. 'Yes—Nikos,' he breathed. 'At last you say my name. And at last, at *last*, this hell is over and we can be together again.' His eyes were washing over her, as if he were reminding himself of every curve, every inch of her.

'*Theos*, but I want you so much...'

He began to pull her against him.

She threw him off. A violent, jerking movement convulsed her.

'Get off me!'

Her voice was shrill. Disbelieving. Panicked.

She took a stumbling step backwards. 'Get out!' The pitch of her voice was higher yet.

He stilled. His tanned chest showed dark against the brilliant white of his open shirtfront.

'*Out?*' He spoke as if she had slapped him.

'Yes—out! Out as in out that door—out! As in get the hell out—as in out! *Out!*'

'You cannot mean that.' His voice was flat. Irrefutable.

As if a note had been struck that hit a resonant frequency the numbness that had wrapped itself around her shattered.

Emotion poured through her as if a dam had burst. Pouring through her like a deluge in her veins.

Her eyes flared.

'What do you mean, I can't mean that? What else should I mean!' She stared at him, transfixed. Her heart had started to beat in huge, ghastly thuds. 'You can't possibly,' she said slowly, her voice strangled, 'you can't *possibly* have thought that this was going to be a marriage in anything other than name only?'

'In name only?' he echoed. He looked at her as if she were the one who was insane. 'Is that what you thought?'

Her face worked. 'Of course it's what I thought! You told me! You told me that it was for Stephanos's and Demetria's sake—because they felt so guilty!'

His eyes flashed with incredulity. 'That did not mean I intended this marriage to be an empty charade! *Theos mou!* It's the only thing that has been keeping me sane! I have been just *aching* to get you back—to take you in my arms again. Make you mine once more!'

He stepped towards her, purpose in his eyes.

'Make love to you again,' he said softly.

She threw her head back. 'Make love?' she bit out. 'We've never made love in our lives!'

He cocked an eyebrow. 'Your memory is so short?' he queried mockingly. He reached for her again. 'Then I must remind you—remind you of each sweet, passionate encounter—each and every time we made love…'

Her face contorted. 'We never made *love*, Nikos! We had sex, that's all. Sex under totally false assumptions—me about you and you about me. That means we never made love—we had sex! When I make love with a man I want

him to know who I am! And I want to know who *he* is too.
Both those conditions were sickeningly absent!'

He dismissed her words as irrelevant sophistry.

'Those conditions no longer apply. And if you think I
wanted you to be the woman I thought you were you must
be mad! Don't you think I rejoiced to discover you weren't
Stephanos's mistress?'

His dark eyes were black, not a speck of gold in them.

Her bosom heaved. 'Of course you rejoiced—it meant
there was no threat to your sister's marriage after all!'

He looked at her, his eyes narrowing dangerously. 'You
really think that was the only reason for my rejoicing?'

'Well, there wasn't much else, was there?' she threw
back at him. 'My God, out of this vile, vile mess that's the
only up side there is!'

She was breathing heavily now; her heart-rate had soared,
her pulse was pounding.

He shook his head. 'Oh, no, Janine. There is another one
too.' He levelled his gaze at her, lambent, sable. 'I get you
back. Back where you belong. In my arms. My bed. I told
you—I have ached and ached for you since you were ripped
from me. Stephanos kept me away from you, and I knew
why and accepted it, even as it drove me mad with frustration—counting, just counting the days, the hours, to this
moment—now. It's been the only thing I've hung on to.'

He took a step towards her. She backed away and found
the wall behind her. Panic was mounting in her. Panic and
another emotion. Stronger, more powerful.

'And now,' said Nikos, as he closed in on her, 'now I
have got you back—'

'No,' she answered, and there was a deadness in her
voice that had not been there a moment ago. 'You won't
lay a finger on me. I couldn't bear you to touch me. Ever
again.'

He stilled.

A long, slow shudder of revulsion passed through her.

'Everything you did to me, everything you said to me was a lie. Right from the start. From the first time you saw me everything was a lie. There was nothing that you did or said to me that was honest! You manipulated me, controlled me, deceived me—*lied* to me from beginning to end! And it was worse than a lie. It was abuse. You deliberately and calculatedly sought my seduction. And I know, with my brain, that you did so in the belief that I was what you and Demetria believed me to be, and that that, to you, justified your actions—but it doesn't make any difference. I feel abused—I *was* abused. It happened.'

'It wasn't like that—' His voice was harsh.

Her face convulsed. Emotion was churning in her. Sick and angry and poisoned.

'It was exactly like that! I know—I was *there*, Nikos! I look back now and I see that every single time you touched me it wasn't *me*. It was a woman you thought capable of having an affair with a married man! A rich married man twenty years older than me! Do you know what that realisation does to me. *Do you?* It makes me want to be sick! Physically sick! And for you to stand there and actually tell me that you want to have sex with me again—that you've been dying for it—makes me feel even sicker!'

Her face convulsed again. 'I'm just a body, aren't I? Just a body! Not a person. You didn't care that I was someone having an affair with a married man—and you don't care that I'm not! You just don't care! Whichever woman I was—or am—doesn't matter to you!'

His hand slashed down through the air.

'That isn't true. I've told you I rejoiced to discover you were never Stephanos's mistress! That you are his daughter.'

'You don't care which one I am. You're perfectly prepared to have sex with either of them!'

He wheeled away from her. 'I don't believe I'm having this conversation.' Emotion stormed through him. What the hell had gone wrong? How the hell had it exploded in his face like this? He turned back to her. 'Listen to me. Out of everything that happened only one thing was true—only one!' His eyes blazed gold. 'This.'

He reached out. His fingers brushed her cheek.

'This.' His other hand slipped around the nape of her neck, stroking with the tips of his fingers.

'This.' He tilted her chin and lowered his mouth to hers.

'This.' He brushed her mouth with his.

For a moment so brief it was less than the space of a single heartbeat she felt the world still.

'*This* was true!' His voice was soft. As soft as velvet. He brushed her lips again with his. As soft as velvet. 'This was always true. That we took one look at each other and wanted each other. That's what we have to remember—only that. Nothing else.'

He was drawing her closer to him. Or moving closer to her. She could not tell. Could only feel herself being pulled into his orbit, powerfully, inexorably. She looked into his eyes. They were glazing over with the blindness of desire. She'd seen it happen so often before, as he became absorbed in a world where only touch existed, only sensation.

It had been the same for her. Every time. *Every time.* She had ceased to think, ceased all mental activity except that of focusing with all her being on the sensations, the exquisite, arousing sensations, of Nikos making love to her…

Ice trickled down her spine.

But he hadn't been making love to her. He'd been having sex with the woman he'd thought was the mistress of a married man. Every time.

That, *that* had been the truth of it. The vile, hideous truth behind the soft words, the softer touch…

Slowly she pulled away.

'Do you know,' she heard herself saying, and her voice was strange—very strange, 'that when you told me just before…just before Stephanos arrived, that you wanted to take me back to Athens with you…do you know what I thought, Nikos?'

She lowered his hands away from her.

'I thought you were asking me to marry you. Isn't that amusing? I thought you were asking me to be your wife. But you weren't, were you? You were taking me to Athens to be your mistress—to make sure I never went back to Stephanos. You were prepared to do that, weren't you Nikos? Prepared to go that far to save your sister's marriage.'

He looked down at her. His face was very strange.

'No,' he said. 'I was prepared to go that far to keep you for myself. I wanted you so much. I want you still so much. I will always want you.'

Her eyes shadowed. 'Whichever woman I am—Stephanos's mistress or his daughter—it doesn't matter. It's just the body that you want.'

A nerve ticked in his cheek.

'I told you that is not true.'

'It has to be!' she hissed. 'It had to be just my body that you wanted—want still. How could you possibly have *made love* to a woman you'd been sent to seduce, deliberately and calculatedly, and then dispose of? Mission complete! Sister's marriage saved!'

'No!' He ran his fingers roughly through his hair. 'No.'

He turned away suddenly. There was tension in every line of his body. He crossed the room, flinging open the wardrobe door and yanking out a cashmere dressing gown. Without looking back he ripped off his shirt, tossing it at a chair, and then dragged on the gown. He belted it with sharp, vicious movements. Then abruptly he turned back to Janine.

For one long, long moment he just looked at her as she stood there across the room, hand clutching the knot of her towel, eyes flashing with hatred for the man who had taken her to bed thinking she was the mistress of a married man, a woman he had been sent to detach from her married lover by any means possible.

Whatever it took.

Including heartbreak.

A sob choked in her throat.

No! Don't think that. Don't. Or you might say it—admit it—and the torment would kill you.

But it was too late. The last, terrible emotion poured from her. The one she had been so desperately, desperately trying to deny—trying to numb as it lay writhing in agony, deep within her wounded self.

Love.

Love for Nikos Kiriakis.

Love for a man who had never looked at her, never touched her, never kissed her or caressed her without seeing her as the woman destroying his sister's marriage, ensnaring his sister's husband. The woman he had been sent to dispose of.

He didn't intend you to fall in love with him...

But she had all the same. She hadn't wanted to, had been fearful of falling for a man like Nikos Kiriakis. But she had embraced it after all, knowing as she did that whatever happened, however brief a time they had, she would be able to treasure her memories of him all her life. Her dreams might never come true, but her memories would always be there.

A laugh bit in her throat. It had no humour in it. Only gall—bitter, bitter gall.

Her memories were false. Each and every one of them.

'I haven't even got my memories,' she said accusingly 'They're false memories. In my every single memory of you you're wearing a mask—hiding from what you saw, a married man's mistress, hiding what you felt—'

'No.' His voice was low, intense. 'It wasn't like that. I wanted you from the moment I laid eyes on you.'

She gave a harsh laugh. 'Well, just as well, I'd say—

wouldn't you? Would have been a bit of a tough challenge having to seduce a woman you didn't fancy!'

The glimmer, the merest glimmer of a mocking smile haunted his mouth. 'That's what I thought.' The smile vanished. 'But it came back to curse me.'

She looked blank. For a long moment he just looked at her, then with a violent gesture ran his hands through his hair. His hands fell to his sides and he rested his eyes on her.

'Your hell started when Stephanos's helicopter landed. Mine started a lot earlier.' He took a deep breath.

Truth time. She wanted truth.

It was all on a knife-edge now. He felt he was standing at the edge of a precipice. And it was going to be her call as to whether she pushed him off the edge or not.

He looked at her. Despite the enveloping towel he could see so much of her. The gentle swell of her breasts. Her slender figure. Her hair tumbling around her beautiful shoulders. The smooth skin of her thighs.

With sheer effort of will he tore his mind away.

It was hard.

Excruciatingly so.

And he knew why. Ever since Stephanos's arrival had turned his world upside down and inside out, sending him hurtling out into the abyss, only one thought had sustained him. That he had to get Janine back.

Because he wanted her, desired her. Whoever she was, whatever she was—mistress, lover, bride.

If he could just get her back everything would be all right. If he could just possess her again everything would be all right. In bed everything would be all right.

Getting her there had become the entire focus of his existence.

I told myself that it was the only truth that had been there all along—the only thing we had emerged with. The only thing that counted.

But he'd been fooling himself.

He went and sat down on the edge of the bed, elbows resting on his knees, and ran his hands through his hair once more. Then he looked up.

Truth time.

For her.

And for him.

His eyes rested on her. She looked so beautiful, so achingly beautiful.

Something churned in him, grinding down through him. The memory of the first moment he'd laid eyes on her leapt in his mind. He saw it—vivid, real.

He'd thought her delectable. So lovely. Spread out there, displaying that soft, sun-kissed body. It had stirred him even then. He remembered his feeling of satisfaction that the mission he'd been sent on would have its compensations. That it would be more than his duty to seduce Janine Fareham—it would his pleasure too.

But it had become much, much more than either.

It had become something he had never, ever before felt for a woman. Women had been for pleasure, that was all. He'd enjoyed them and kissed them goodbye, moved on to the next one.

But Janine—

He had felt the danger. He couldn't even deny that, whatever else he denied. From the moment he'd set eyes on her! Felt it and dismissed it! He remembered standing on the balcony of Stephanos's hotel on Skarios, thinking how captivating she was. The word had made him alarmed, he realised. He'd argued around it mentally and had applied it to Janine instead. That *she'd* be captivated. That way he'd felt safe.

Fool! Fool to think that he could just reassign words— feelings—to other people!

Fool to simply ignore what had been happening to him.

Ignore everything about Janine Fareham except the need to seduce her.

Ignore everything except his desire for her.

Fool.

Psychologists had a phrase for it. Displacement activity.

Something you did instead of doing what you wanted to do. Because there was such a block against doing what you wanted to do that you couldn't do it. So you did something else instead.

Well, that was what he had done. He had done something else instead. He'd focused totally and absolutely on the one thing that he'd known he could do with Janine Fareham. He could desire her, and he could seduce her, and he could get her into bed with him and possess her utterly.

And once he had possessed her he would keep her.

Whatever happened he would keep her.

He would do anything, but he would keep her.

And when she was taken away from him, as Stephanos had taken her, then he would do anything to get her back.

And that was just what he'd done. He'd married her.

But he hadn't got her back.

He looked across at her. She stood there so beautiful. Achingly beautiful.

And as remote as a shining, distant star.

Hell closed over him. The same hell that had started the moment he had first laid eyes on her. He hadn't known it—couldn't possibly have known it. But he had walked into it all the same. Step by step.

He had been seducing her. Step by step. And all the while—all the while she had been seducing him. Not his senses, but a far, far more powerful part of his being.

His heart.

His eyes rested on her still. She hadn't spoken, hadn't moved. How long had he been silent? He didn't know. Couldn't tell.

'My hell...' he said, and his voice was very strange. 'My hell started when I fell in love with the woman who was breaking up my sister's marriage.'

CHAPTER NINE

HE HAD said it. Said a word that had come out of nowhere. Shocking him to the core. Shocking him because he had known the moment it came out of his mouth that it was true.

He hadn't known he was going to say it. Any more than he'd known he was going to do it.

Or realised that it had happened.

Why? he thought, with a weird, dissociated sense of strangeness. Why had it happened? It was an alien word to him—totally alien. It had never been part of his life, not with any of his partners. He'd never wanted it to be and he'd never even entertained the idea of falling in love.

It had been unnecessary and he'd never even thought about it.

And so, he realised, with a sinking, deadly hollowness, he had not recognised it.

I called it desire.

But it was love.

Love all along.

The shock of it buckled through him.

And in the wake of shock, in the slipstream left behind it, pain lanced him like a spear thrown with lethal, mortal accuracy.

Unrequited love.

Because what else could it be? Hadn't she made it clear? After what he'd done to her—even though he hadn't meant to—how could she feel anything for him but loathing?

'I can't bear your touch!' He'd heard her say it—her voice shuddering with revulsion.

He'd tried to sweep it aside. Wanted only to push past

her defences and dissolve her resistance to him, make her see, feel, that the only thing they must focus on was on the one good thing that had come out of this sorry, sordid mess. That in each other's arms nothing else mattered. Not whether or not she was Stephanos's mistress. Not whether or not he had been sent to ensure her defection from his sister's husband.

Just each other.

But she hadn't seen it that way.

She had been revolted by what had happened between them. Revolted by the lie, revolted by what he had thought her then.

Slowly his head sank into his hands.

Despair took him over.

There was a soft footfall on the carpet, a shadow falling over him. A scent of soap and body cream—and Janine. Her own scent, that sweet bouquet that he would have recognised anywhere—in the dark, on the moon…anywhere.

Fingers smoothed his hair.

'Oh, Nikos.'

Her voice was soft. As soft as her silken skin. As soft as her sweet breasts.

She knelt down beside him, her hand slipping from his head to rest on his knee.

He turned his bowed head towards her.

She was so close, so *close*. Her lips were parted, her eyes wide and luminous.

He couldn't help himself. Dear God, but he could not help himself.

His mouth reached for hers blindly, instinctively.

She let him kiss her, let his mouth move and taste hers. And then slowly, oh, so slowly, she started to kiss him back.

He gathered her up to him, drawing her down on the bed beside him. The towel had loosened and he felt her breasts pressing against him. His eyes had shut. He did not want to see, only to feel. To feel the bliss, the sheer bliss, of having Janine in his arms again.

He had ached for her. With his body. With his heart.

His hands stroked over her as his mouth went on and on, kissing and kissing her. If he died now, this moment, it would be enough.

Her fingers were at his waist, loosening the tie of his robe, smoothing over his chest, his flanks. He laid her down on the bed, his hands slipping to her breasts, shaping and caressing them. He could feel the beat of her heart, the soft rise and fall of her lungs.

'Janine—'

His voice was a husk. A plea.

She placed her fingers over his lips.

'Shh—no words. No words.'

She slipped her fingers away to let her lips graze along his jaw, his neck, arching her spine towards him. Her legs were easing along his, her other hand smoothing over his back, along each muscled ridge.

He felt himself surge against her, and realised, feeling the exquisite, arousing *frottage*, that he was still in his shorts.

He groaned, and he felt her smile against his throat.

Wordlessly she eased them from him, her hands coming back to cup over the tensing muscles of his buttocks. He surged again, his flesh seeking hers. Blindly, instinctively.

Sinking within her was paradise. Paradise, and heaven, and home.

Such paradise that he did it again, and again, and yet again.

He felt her head begin to thresh, felt her mouth leave his, her neck arch. Heard, felt all the way through him, the low, vibrating moan that started in her throat and built all through her body, all through his, building and building until his whole body was resonating with hers in one perfect, endless harmony.

She came as he did. He could feel her peak, pulse all around him, slow and deep and heavy and endless. As endless as the rush that came as his seed filled her and filled her.

He gathered her close to him, as close as his heart, enfolding her even as he finished surging within her, even as she still softly pulsed around him. His arms wrapped around her, his cheek was against hers, and he lifted her from the bed to embrace her, so close to him, so close.

A great lassitude filled him. Slackening all his limbs, loosening all his muscles. She slipped from him, her weight pressing heavy against him. Heavy and warm and soft, so soft. He pillowed his head upon her breasts and felt her stroke his hair, her fingers sifting, soothing.

Peace filled him. A peace so profound, so absolute, that it stilled him utterly as he lay there, enfolded and enfolding. His mouth formed one more soft kiss against her breast, and then sleep, sweet sleep, came at last and took him in.

For a long, long time she held him, tears seeping through her lashes.

And in the morning she was gone.

He woke, instantly knowing something was wrong. Desperately, appallingly wrong.

Janine was not there.

Like a terrible yawning chasm her absence swallowed him, devouring him. He clawed around him, as if he might feel her suddenly there, back again.

But she was gone. Gone.

Pain clutched at him.

I thought I had her back! I thought I had her back!

Black agony sawed through him.

He forced his eyes open. Forced himself to see her absence. See her not there. Not there.

Not her, nor her bag, nor her shoes or her clothes, nor any part of her.

Nothing of her. Nothing.

The emptiness of the room was everywhere, inside him and outside him. She had left him. She had gone. He had not won her back. Could never win her back.

No hope. None.

With eyes like death he got out of bed, groping for the bathrobe that she had peeled from his body when she had taken him back—back to that paradise that came only in her arms. Only hers.

Pain scissored through him. A lifetime of pain waiting to devour him, day by day. Without her. Without Janine. The woman he loved—and could not win back.

He slid his arms down into the robe's sleeves, yanking the belt across him.

And froze.

There on the chest of drawers, propped up against the wall, was a piece of folded paper. Dread filled him. This was it, then. This was the final moment when he would see, in words, her absolute rejection of him.

He crossed the space in a second, seizing up the paper, opening it with rapid fumbling fingers. The words blurred, resolved, and blurred again.

Then cleared.

And as he read them a gratitude so profound went through him that he wanted to fall to his knees.

She had not left him.

The paper shook in his hands but the words held steady. Shining true and faithful. Filling him with the one thing he craved above all now.

Hope.

He stared again at what she had written.

'In our end is our beginning.'

He set down the paper, looking up. His eyes saw far. Very far. As far as the woman he loved. Words moved on his lips. Silently. Lovingly.

I am coming to you, my beloved. I am coming to you.

* * *

Janine eased herself over onto her stomach and sighed languorously, giving her body to the sun. In front of her the sunlight danced dazzlingly off the azure swimming pool. Beyond, slender cypresses pierced the cerulean sky.

The sound of children splashing and calling in the pool was the only noise. She felt the warmth of the sun like a blessing on her naked back.

A shadow fell over her.

'*Kyria* Fareham?'

She looked up, twisting her head round.

Her breath caught.

She was looking at the most devastating male she had ever seen in her life.

Sable hair feathered across a broad brow, strong and straight, with deep lines curving from it to the edges of his mouth.

His mouth—

Sculpted. That was the only word for it. With a sensuous lower lip she had to drag her eyes from, forcing herself to meet his eyes instead. Dark eyes, flecked with gold. And blazing down at her with an emotion that made her feel weak with its strength.

She felt the world shift around her, then resettle.

As if something had changed for ever.

He had asked her a question, she realised, and she must answer it. But she must be cautious. So much, so very, very much, was at stake.

'Who wants to know?' she asked softly.

That same overpowering, overwhelming emotion blazed from those dark, devastating eyes.

'The man who loves her,' answered Nikos Kiriakis. 'The man who loves her and will always love her, to the end of our days.'

He held out a hand for her and she placed hers in it. It closed over hers, warm and safe. He drew her up.

'Why did you come here?' she asked, in that same soft voice.

His eyes rested on her.

'*"In our end is our beginning."'*

A smile parted her lips. It lit her face.

'You understood—?'

He nodded. 'Yes. When I woke to find you gone my first thought was despair. You had left me. And then...' His voice changed. 'Then I saw the note that you had left behind. "In our end is our beginning." And I knew what you were trying to tell me.'

He took a deep breath, gazing down at her. 'You wanted us to start again. To undo, unmake all that had gone before and make it again. Just you and I. Meeting, desiring, loving. Nothing else. The way it should have been.' He lowered his head, gently grazing her mouth with his. 'The way it always will be now.'

A deep, deep joy filled her. A happiness so profound it made her weak with the wonder of it. She felt the tears start in her eyes.

'Nikos. Oh, Nikos!'

He held her tight, so very tight, crushing her against him. But for a few, brief seconds only. Then, carefully, he set her back. She gazed up at him. Love blazed in her eyes.

He smiled down at her. Something moved in his eyes, blazed forth like her love, and then, with long lashes sweeping down, veiled itself.

'I wonder, *Kyria* Fareham,' he said in a courteous voice, 'whether you might like to take a little cruise? Not far. Just along the coast. I've a villa there you might like to see.'

She tilted her head slightly. 'Does it have an infinity pool?'

'It does.'

'And wonderful sea views?'

'Indeed.'

'Sunsets?'

'Fabulous sunsets.'

'Is it very private?'

'Completely private.'

She paused a moment. 'How many bedrooms?'

A smile quirked at his mouth. 'I never bothered to count. But we,' he told her, 'shall be using only one.'

He took her hand. 'And it hasn't,' he told her, 'got twin beds.'

She slid her fingers into his.

'Sounds irresistible.'

His free hand cupped her cheek.

'Then don't resist. Don't resist anything.' The flecks of gold in his eyes burned molten. 'Especially,' he murmured, 'me.'

She felt her body melt against him.

'Never,' she answered. 'For the rest of our lives.'

'Good,' said Nikos Kiriakis. And kissed her.

As their bodies moved and fused in the dim light of the shuttered room, the cool air playing over their skin, and they took each other to that one private paradise which only they inhabited, it was as if nothing that had gone before had ever happened. It was all made new between them.

And afterwards, in the peace that came only after loving, she spoke, cradled safe in his arms. At last so safe.

'It hurt so much that you could think such a thing of me. Something so vile and horrible. For the first time since Stephanos had taken me into his heart as his daughter the reality of my Greek heritage was starting to take root. And you were part of it! Part of the country I was trying to feel a part of. You had swept me away, made me feel so wonderful! I had woven such dreams about you, such longing fantasies—that you would take me back to Athens, declare your love for me to Stephanos, and we would all live happily ever after.... And then to find out, like that, what you really thought of me. Had thought of me all along.'

Her voice gave a little choke and he crushed her to him even closer, anguished at her anguish. She went on speaking, draining the poison from her.

'I couldn't bear it. Just couldn't bear it. I knew with my head that you had had every reason to think ill of me—that everything had been a hideous, terrible misunderstanding! And neither of us had realised! You talked about my relationship with Stephanos and I thought it meant you knew I was his daughter! And all along you thought I was…I was his mistress! You thought I lived off his money, that I didn't even work for a living and never had! And that wasn't true either. I mean, I did work. But not for money.'

She took a deep, shuddering breath. 'You see, when my mother died I inherited her money. She was never poor—she always had a private income—but she used her money simply to flit around on the Côte d'Azur, wasting her life away in one long, endless holiday. I vowed I would never lead such a pointless life. So I went to the opposite extreme and went to work for a Third World agency. Louise—my mother—thought I was mad, but she was glad to see the back of me. She didn't want a grown-up daughter making her look old. When I inherited her money I could work for the agency for free. And for the last three years I've been working for them abroad. It was gruelling, but so incredibly worthwhile! I chose to work abroad, in some terrible, heartbreaking places, but in the end I reached burnout. I'd just arrived back in London, feeling guilty for not having been able to cope any more, and that's when I met Stephanos.

'It was a miracle! A complete miracle! My mother had never told me about my father. Hadn't been in the least interested. And since she'd died I'd accepted—I'd had to accept!—that I'd never, ever know. But Stephanos—he simply took me to him. Took me into his life, into his heart. Without question. And him being rich was another miracle. He's settled so much money on me that I can support the aid agency I used to work for so much better than I could before. But…' She hesistated, then went on. 'But I know that the life I led sheltered me from…from men. The kind of men that Louise surrounded herself with. Rich and glamorous. Like you.' She closed her eyes. 'I didn't want to be tempted by you. But I was. I couldn't resist you. I just couldn't! So—so I gave in to you. I fell for you totally. Completely. Then…then when Stephanos arrived it was like a nightmare. And I felt…I felt I was being punished—rightfully—for having been such a prize idiot as to fall for a man like you.'

She gave a long, shuddering sigh. 'I hated you. I hated you for thinking such vile things about me—that I was Stephanos's mistress—the kind of woman my mother was, who thought nothing of having an affair with a married man!—and I hated you because I'd fallen in love with you.'

He smoothed her hair tenderly, with a hand that was not quite steady.

She lifted her head from where it had lain on his chest, his heart beating beneath her cheek. She looked at him suddenly, urgently.

'But it's all right now—it's all right now, isn't it, Nikos? Isn't it?'

He kissed her softly, cradling her head.

'Yes,' he breathed. 'It's all right now. It's all right—and from now on it will always, always be all right. Because we are together. We've found each other—the people we truly are. No more lies.' He kissed each eyelid, each corner of her mouth. 'We've made our new beginning.'

She smiled into his mouth, deep, deep peace filling her.

'In our beginning is our end?'

'Yes,' said Nikos. 'Oh, yes.'

And he kissed her, slow and deep and full of love.

EPILOGUE

'SMILE! One more time! All four of you!'

Nikos raised the camera and focused through the lens once more.

His sister made a face. 'They're too young to smile! They don't smile until at least three months!'

'And then the books say it's usually wind!' added her stepdaughter for good measure.

'Then you two smile!' ordered Nikos.

Demetria sat up a little straighter and fussed over her son's magnificent christening robe. Beside her, on the sofa, Janine smoothed the head of *her* son—and rearranged him slightly in her arms. The two women glanced at each other, sudden tears filling their eyes.

Tears of happiness. Sheer happiness.

Demetria took Janine's hand.

'I beat you to it,' she said in a low voice. 'I was determined to do so!'

Janine pressed the other woman's hand, feeling her joy, her relief. Demetria had longed so much, and so long, for a child of her own.

When she'd first realised she was pregnant, less than six months into her marriage, Janine had been torn between joy and anguish. For close on two months she and Nikos had kept it a closely guarded secret, dreading the time when Demetria would have to know that her sister-in-law was to bear her brother a child, a grandchild to her own husband.

And then, during the Easter celebrations, Stephanos had drawn his wife to her feet.

'We have something to tell you,' he had said to his daughter and his son-in-law—his brother-in-law.

He placed a proud, protective hand over Demetria's stomach.

'Our child is growing here,' he said. 'Through the miracle of science he lives and grows.'

'We didn't want to say anything,' said Demetria, her voice full with emotion, 'not until the first trimester was over and we knew the pregnancy was secure.'

Janine rushed to embrace her, and as her arms folded around her sister-in-law—her stepmother—she heard Demetria say, 'And now, my dearest Janine, you can tell me why you will drink no wine, and have a glow about you that I see only in my own mirror!'

It had been a race from then on. A race that Demetria had been determined to win.

'I have a secret advantage,' she'd told Janine smugly. 'One of the nicest things about assisted conception is that you know exactly what day your baby is conceived! That means my due date is as accurate as it can be! As for you…' She'd looked with mock resignation at her brother's wife. 'If you can know which night Nikos gave you your child, then all that billing and cooing you do all the time will have been a most unlikely lie!'

Janine had coloured, and Nikos had looked even more smug than his sister.

Now, with both babies successfully delivered, both mothers recovered from childbed, the two women sat, posing themselves and their offspring while yet more photos were taken.

On the other side of the room Stephanos sat back in his comfortable chair. Champagne beaded in his glass. His eyes were suspiciously wet.

As his brother-in-law, his son-in-law, finally lowered his camera, Stephanos raised his glass again.

'One more toast!' he cried.

Nikos set down his camera and picked up his glass. The

two men raised their glasses. Two pairs of eyes rested on
the women sitting on the sofa, their babies on their laps.

'To happiness,' said Stephanos. His voice was thick with
emotion. 'To my daughter and my wife. My son and my
grandson. May this day be blessed.'

'I think,' said Nikos, as his eyes rested on Janine and
hers on him, and the lovelight blazed from both of them,
'it already is.'

And then, quite suddenly, his eyes were suspiciously
wet too.

INTERNATIONAL DOCTORS

They're guaranteed
to raise your pulse!

Meet the most eligible medical men of the world,
in a series of stories by popular authors that
will make your heart race!

Whether they're saving lives or dealing with desire,
our doctors have bedside manners that
send temperatures soaring....

Coming in November 2005:

THE ITALIAN DOCTOR'S MISTRESS

by Catherine Spencer

#2503

Pick up a Harlequin Presents® novel and you will enter a world
of spine-tingling passion and provocative, tantalizing romance!

Available wherever Harlequin books are sold.

HARLEQUIN®
Presents

Seduction and Passion Guaranteed!

www.eHarlequin.com

HPTIDM

Christmas comes to

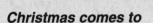

In November 2005, don't miss:

MISTLETOE MARRIAGE
(#3869)

by Jessica Hart

For Sophie Beckwith, this Christmas means
facing the ex who dumped her and then married
her sister! Only one person can help: her best friend
Bram. Bram used to be engaged to Sophie's sister,
and now, determined to show the lovebirds that
they've moved on, he's come up with a plan: he's
proposed to Sophie!

Then in December look out for:

CHRISTMAS GIFT: A FAMILY
(#3873)

by Barbara Hannay

Happy with his life as a wealthy bachelor,
Hugh Strickland is stunned to discover he has
a daughter. He wants to bring Ivy home—but he's
absolutely terrified! Hugh hardly knows Jo Berry,
but he pleads with her to help him—surely the ideal
solution would be to give each other the perfect
Christmas gift: a family....

Available wherever Harlequin books are sold.

www.eHarlequin.com   HRXMAS

If you enjoyed what you just read,
then we've got an offer you can't resist!

Take 2 bestselling love stories FREE!

Plus get a FREE surprise gift!

Clip this page and mail it to Harlequin Reader Service®

IN U.S.A.	IN CANADA
3010 Walden Ave.	P.O. Box 609
P.O. Box 1867	Fort Erie, Ontario
Buffalo, N.Y. 14240-1867	L2A 5X3

YES! Please send me 2 free Harlequin Presents® novels and my free surprise gift. After receiving them, if I don't wish to receive anymore, I can return the shipping statement marked cancel. If I don't cancel, I will receive 6 brand-new novels every month, before they're available in stores! In the U.S.A., bill me at the bargain price of $3.80 plus 25¢ shipping & handling per book and applicable sales tax, if any*. In Canada, bill me at the bargain price of $4.47 plus 25¢ shipping & handling per book and applicable taxes**. That's the complete price and a savings of at least 10% off the cover prices—what a great deal! I understand that accepting the 2 free books and gift places me under no obligation ever to buy any books. I can always return a shipment and cancel at any time. Even if I never buy another book from Harlequin, the 2 free books and gift are mine to keep forever.

106 HDN DZ7Y
306 HDN DZ7Z

Name	(PLEASE PRINT)	
Address	Apt.#	
City	State/Prov.	Zip/Postal Code

Not valid to current Harlequin Presents® subscribers.

Want to try two free books from another series?
Call 1-800-873-8635 or visit www.morefreebooks.com.

* Terms and prices subject to change without notice. Sales tax applicable in N.Y.
** Canadian residents will be charged applicable provincial taxes and GST.
All orders subject to approval. Offer limited to one per household.
® are registered trademarks owned and used by the trademark owner and or its licensee.

PRES04R   ©2004 Harlequin Enterprises Limited

eHARLEQUIN.com
The Ultimate Destination for Women's Fiction

Your favorite authors are just a click away
at www.eHarlequin.com!

- Take a sneak peek at the covers and
  read summaries of **Upcoming Books**

- Choose from over 600
  author **profiles!**

- Chat with your favorite authors
  on our **message boards.**

- Are you an author in the making?
  Get advice from published authors
  in **The Inside Scoop!**

**Learn about your favorite authors
in a fun, interactive setting—
visit www.eHarlequin.com today!**

INTAUTH04R

Coming Next Month

THE BEST HAS JUST GOTTEN BETTER!

#2499 THE DISOBEDIENT VIRGIN Sandra Marton
The Ramirez Brides
Catarina Mendes has been dictated to all her life. Now, with her
twenty-first birthday, comes freedom—but it's freedom at a price.
Jake Ramirez has become her guardian. He must find a man for her to
marry. But Jake is so overwhelmed by her beauty that he is tempted to
keep Cat for himself...

#2500 SALE OR RETURN BRIDE Sarah Morgan
For Love or Money
Sebastien Fiorukis is to marry Alesia Philipos. Their families have been
feuding for generations, but it seems finally the rift is healed. However,
all is not as it seems. Alesia has been bought by her husband—and
she will *not* be a willing wife!

#2501 THE GREEK'S BOUGHT WIFE Helen Bianchin
Wedlocked!
Nic Leandros knows that people are only after his money. So when he
finds that beautiful Tina Matheson is pregnant with his late brother's
child, he's certain her price will be high. Tina must agree to his terms:
they will marry for the baby's sake...

#2502 PREGNANCY OF REVENGE Jacqueline Baird
Bedded by Blackmail
Charlotte Summerville was a gold digger according to billionaire
Jake d'Amato and he planned to take revenge in his bed! Suddenly
innocent Charlie was married to a man who wanted her, but hated
her...and she was pregnant with his child...

#2503 THE ITALIAN DOCTOR'S MISTRESS Catherine Spencer
International Doctors
Successful neurosurgeon Carlo Rossi has a passion for his work—and
for women. And he desires Danielle Blake like no other woman. He
insists they play by his rules—no future, just a brief affair. But when
it's time for Danielle to leave Italy can he let her go?

#2504 BOUND BY BLACKMAIL Kate Walker
The Alcolar Family
Jake Taverner wants Mercedes Alcolar. So when she rejects him in
the most painful way, his hurt pride demands revenge. Jake traps
Mercedes into a fake engagement and embarks on a skillful seduction.
But though he can bind her by blackmail...can he keep her?

HPCNM1005